Praise for *The Astronomer*

"Biswas is a master storyteller who pulls the reader into a journey of epic proportions." – *The BookLife Prize*

"Biswas' writing is remarkably expansive throughout, and readers will find it deeply impressive how he captures two distinct voices: one of prosaic reason and another of disordered brilliance. Overall, it's a fantastically strange novel that's as grippingly eccentric as the protagonist at its center." – *Kirkus Reviews*

"In Brian Biswas' novel, *The Astronomer*, he has chosen to confound us frequently regarding how he and the main character regard reality, and we are often forced to think about our own ways of looking at the real and the fantastic, about fact and fiction. . . . He also challenges us to think about whether or not the dreams and other mental wanderings of people who don't have 'normal' mental lives constitute another reality as well." – *The Cafe Irreal*

"This thoughtful, uncompromisingly literary voyage is for lovers of science, prose touched with poetry, and life at the edges—of the mind, of the universe." – *BookLife*

"Two readers can walk away from this book with different readings, different realities, but each of them will be thinking." – *The Starving Artist*

The Astronomer

Also by Brian Biswas

A Betrayal and Other Stories

Brian Biswas

THE
ASTRONOMER

WHISKEY TIT
NYC & VT

Published in the United States and Canada by Whisk(e)y Tit: www.whiskeytit.com. If you wish to use or reproduce all or part of this book for any means, please let the author and publisher know. You're pretty much required to, legally.

ISBN 978-1-952600-31-9
Library of Congress Control Number: 2023904860

To Elizabeth, as always

TABLE OF CONTENTS

Preface		1
PART ONE		
I	The Moons of Jupiter	11
II	Jason and the Argonauts	25
III	The Rings of Saturn	45
IV	The Black Hole	59
V	Many Happy Returns	71
VI	There Is No Life on Mars	95
VII	The Distance to the Galaxies	113
INTERLUDE		
Gods and Goddesses		131
PART TWO		
VIII	Home on the Range	139
IX	New Methods of Space Travel	155
X	I'm Still Here!	177
XI	Journey to Andromeda	201
XII	The Displaced Man	217
XIII	The Last Photon	229
Postscript		237
About the Author		253
About the Publisher		255

The Astronomer

PREFACE

ON THE ELDERLY MAN WHO FREQUENTED THE PEORIA ASTRONOMICAL SOCIETY AND WHAT BECAME OF HIM

I first saw Franz Herbert at a meeting of the Peoria Astronomical Society in April of 1962. I was teaching comparative literature at the University of Illinois at Urbana-Champaign and had traveled to Peoria to attend the monthly meetings of the society, astronomy being a keen interest of mine.

The society met in the meeting room of an old church on Perry Avenue. Herbert always sat in the same place, on a wooden chair in the back near a corner window. He was a middle-aged man, probably in his mid-fifties, with thinning brown hair, blue eyes, a face that was both pitted and lined. He had a sorrowful expression, as if he had suffered much in life.

It was during one such meeting, near the end of a lecture on Saturn's moon Titan, when there was a loud commotion from the street outside. I jumped up, rushed to the window, and looked out. There had been an ugly car crash, directly across from the church: a red Mercedes and a white Buick station wagon had collided head-on. A police car was already at the scene and in the distance I heard the wail of an ambulance. I found myself standing next to Herbert, who had not risen from his seat. After expressing my concern about the condition of the drivers, I made some banal comment about people not paying attention and he nodded.

From that point on, Herbert never failed to smile when he saw me arrive. One time—I think it was in August—he approached after the meeting, drink in hand. He told me that he had once taught astronomy at a university on the east coast but was retired. His nights were spent observing under Illinois' starry sky. As for his days . . . His words trailed off. Herbert's voice was deep and resonant; it must have been quite a treat to listen to his lectures on the heavens.

I told him I myself was a college professor. And then I inquired about his daytime occupation.

"Writing my memoirs," he said with a wry smile. "The story of a sordid life."

I chuckled. I said I, too, was a writer, and asked if he hoped to publish his work. He replied that one day he just might.

I missed the next several meetings—I was writing a biography of James Joyce for which my publisher was getting impatient—and when I returned to Peoria in December, I saw no sign of Herbert. My inquiries met with shrugs. That should have been that, I suppose, but I could not stop thinking about the man, his odd way of speaking, his airy, wistful expression, the air of otherworldliness that seemed to hang about him.

As luck would have it, I came upon him a month later, in a bar on the west side of Peoria. He was sitting in a dimly-lit corner, observing customers as they came and went. Occasionally he would write something on a napkin (there was a stack on the table), then fold it in two and place it in his breast pocket.

I approached and asked if I could join him. He smiled and pulled out a chair.

When I mentioned my concern at his disappearance, he broke into a hearty laugh. "Just needed to take a break," he said. Then he began talking about the stars and the "gods and goddesses who rule over all."

I raised an eyebrow.

Before another word was said, the door creaked open and a young couple entered. Herbert looked across the room and I saw that his eyes were shimmering like starlight.

"The world thinks I'm crazy, I know," he said, turning back to face me. "A demented, though harmless, man. And all because I can go where they cannot!"

I had no idea what he was talking about, and had a feeling I was treading into territory best left unexplored, but I asked anyway, "What do you mean?"

Herbert looked befuddled, as if he wasn't sure how much to confide. Then he said, "The world is composed of momentary, unconnected fragments. I, being of the world, am likewise composed. Consider a mirror. A mirror which reflects in its image the portrait of a man. One day the mirror explodes and hundreds of fragments are scattered about. They are carefully reassembled until the mirror once again shows the man's image. But there are many ways to piece a mirror back together. Which one of them is true? And does the question itself even have meaning?"

His thoughts were fodder for philosophical speculation, I supposed, but I had no idea what to make of them. I wondered, though, if perhaps the man had suffered a tragedy in the past—his world exploding—one from which he never fully recovered.

I had to excuse myself at this point for the hour was late and I needed to return to Urbana without further delay. I had an 8 A.M. lecture the next day and had yet to prepare my notes. I fully intended to continue my conversations with Herbert, but I never saw or heard from him again.

Several years later I received a call from a Dr. Arnold, who said he was Herbert's psychiatrist. He wondered if I might be interested in perusing Herbert's manuscript, entitled *The Astronomer*, which had been found on his bedside table. Herbert himself had vanished, leaving only these traces behind, along with a request that in the event of his disappearance they be delivered to me. I responded affirmatively, telling him I had been intrigued by the man's enigmatic nature.

The work consists of sixteen diary entries—the diaries themselves have never been found—reflections by Herbert on life and his place in the world, along with chapters from an apparent memoir. Herbert did not number the chapters. He did, however, have the odd habit of repeating the final words of one chapter at the beginning of the next. This may have been the order intended. In any event, it is the order I followed. I interspersed the diary entries between chapters as seemed appropriate and added this preface which strikes me as superfluous but which I will let stand for historical reasons. Also included is an account of Herbert's life as told by his psychiatrist Dr. Joseph Arnold.

This, then, is Herbert's story.

Professor Martin Pasqual

My mother had a sheet
That she could never fold;
My father had more silver coins
Than he could ever hold.
What were they?

—Ancient Mexican riddle

PART

ONE

THE VEIL OF THE SWAN

(May 12, 1927)

I discovered an object the other day which I have named the Lost Comet Swan. I could have named it the Lost Ghost Comet for it looks like a wraith flying across the heavens. It is hurtling towards Vega in the constellation Lyra and in thirty-three years and seven months the star will gobble it up.

I have never seen a comet in interstellar space and I wonder: where did it come from? Vega is one of the closer stars to Earth, only twenty-five light years distant. I get out my sky charts and protractor and calculate. I find that a comet with the Lost Comet Swan's characteristics did indeed orbit the sun many years ago. It had been pulled off course and was heading out of the solar system towards the Summer Triangle wherein Vega lies. (Vega means "the swooping eagle" so perhaps that had something to do with it.) Vega is a rapidly rotating star with its axis pointed towards Earth. It is a stellar tractor beam that is slowly pulling in its prey: the Lost Comet Swan.

The head of the Lost Comet Swan shines with a brilliant white light. The coma surrounding the head glows with an eerie green hue. What fascinates me most, though, is the tail. It is the longest cometary tail I have ever seen, extending out for thousands of miles. A great cosmic veil. And it is the tail that gives the Lost Comet Swan its ghostly appearance.

The tail has another interesting property—it oscillates time. By this I mean the following: if you place yourself within the tail, time sweeps over you in waves. Imagine immersing yourself in the ocean, waves crashing down on you —it is this sensation. Only not of water but of time.

It is disorienting, to say the least, for you don't know to which time period you truly belong. I was terrified by what I experienced in these cosmic oscillations:

I was present at the birth of creation.

I was there when the universe no longer existed.

I saw the whiteness of birth and the blackness of death.

I saw the paleness of all that was in between.

I witnessed the march of human history:

    Caesar is murdered.

        Christ is crucified.

            Genghis Khan rules the earth.

                Einstein unravels the Cosmos.

                    Franz Herbert is diagnosed with epilepsy.

I

THE MOONS OF JUPITER

When the doctor told me I had epilepsy, I was shocked. I'd suspected something might be wrong. I heard voices. I was other places. But never this. This most hideous of diseases. This could never happen to me. There was no history of epilepsy in my family. I had never suffered from seizures or auras of any type. I was twenty years old and I had my entire life ahead of me. Perhaps the doctor was mistaken? But, alas, subsequent tests confirmed the original diagnosis: petite mal seizures that would only worsen over time unless immediate action was taken.

The doctor gave me pills that turned the walls of my bedroom many colors. They pulsated. They bled. One sultry August night—the year was 1926, the year Arthur Eddington published *The Internal Constitution of the Stars*—I clung to my girlfriend, Isabella, as I felt my mind beginning to swoon and then convulse. We were in the backyard of my parent's home in Peoria, Illinois, gazing up at the constellations, and suddenly the firmament came crashing down upon me and I was drowning in light.

Oh my God, I thought. You are going to die.

* * *

An epileptic's life is no fun, let me tell you. For one thing you never know where you are. You could be here. You could be there. And in reality you're neither place—or rather, you're in both places simultaneously. Twilight worlds that flash in and out of existence.

I was passed from physician to physician. No one knew what to do with me. The diagnoses multiplied, the prescriptions multiplied, but my condition only worsened. Eventually I ended up in a local hospital. I was filled with so many drugs I didn't know who I was or who I had ever been. A specialist from University Medical Center examined me and to my amazement he took me off all medication. "There is nothing wrong with you," he said. "It's all in your mind."

I said, somewhat sarcastically, "Of course it's in my mind."

But he was right—it was all in my mind—and when I realized this I began to recover.

I learned to control my epilepsy.

And then I learned to control other things.

* * *

Galileo Galilei did not discover the moons of Jupiter in January 1610 as history has recorded. The German astronomer Simon Marius did—in November 1609. Marius, however, never published his observations, mentioning them only to his friend Johannes Kepler, who wrote of them in his memoirs many years later. Galileo made extensive observations and published them in the journal *Sidereus Nuncius* in March 1610. In 1614, Marius did provide what would one day become the names of the Jovian moons, based on a suggestion from Kepler.

* * *

"Jupiter," Marius wrote, "is much blamed by the poets on account of his irregular loves. Three maidens are especially mentioned as having been clandestinely courted by Jupiter with success. Io, daughter of the River; Callisto, daughter of Lycaon; and Europa of Agenor. Then there was Ganymede, the handsome son of King Tros, whom Jupiter, having taken the form of an eagle, transported to heaven on his back. . . . I think, therefore, that I shall not be amiss if I call the First Io, the Second Europa, the Third, on account of its majesty of light, Ganymede, the Fourth Callisto. . . ."

* * *

The first moon I came upon was Callisto, the outermost of the Galilean satellites and the only one to orbit beyond Jupiter's radiation belts. Callisto is the third largest moon in the solar system (but not the largest Galilean moon; that honor goes to Ganymede) and is about the size of the planet Mercury. It is the darkest of Jupiter's moons and is the most heavily cratered object in the solar system. Its surface age is estimated to be four billion years.

I put down near Lofn, a shallow, circular crater about sixty-two miles across. Callisto has no atmosphere and so I put on my space suit and emerged from the ship, gently stepping out onto the oldest landscape in the solar system. I traveled along the Adlinda Basin, following the curve of the crater.

Now if you've never been to Callisto, you will want to listen closely. Many of Adlinda's features are obscured by ejecta from the crater. The ejecta covers an older, more densely cratered surface that includes sinuous ridges and fractures. There is a saltwater ocean deep inside Callisto that is reached by means of a channel found at the bottom of one of these fractures. It is a two-day hike through splendid geologic formations: thermal vents, sulfuric lakes, and enormous ice sculptures. And it was when I reached the ocean that I began my search for Callisto, the daughter of Lycaeon, for she was known to inhabit this region of the moon. I doubt that I will ever find her, though. Probably she died in this godforsaken place out of sheer loneliness. (And who could blame her?) At one point I see what looks like a winged deer flying overhead—the bluish-green antlers are magnificent—but it might have been my imagination.

* * *

Epilepsy is a disorder of the brain, specifically excessive electrical activity of nerve cells. There are two main seizure types. In the most dramatic, known as grand mal seizures, the subject loses consciousness, falls to the ground, shakes violently, and becomes stiff. He may become blue in the lips and foam at the mouth. I have never had one of these seizures. There is another type, known as petite mal seizures, in which there is simple alteration of consciousness without the theatrics. With grand mal seizures there is often a warning of seizure onset: for example, an olfactory, visual or auditory hallucination, or a sensation of pain or nausea. With petite mal seizures there is usually no warning, and in my case there is no warning. Isabella tells me that I appear to lose consciousness, but that the loss is brief, that I stare straight ahead, blink, fidget with my hands, and sometimes appear nervous. This is not the way I perceive it. Rather, I feel that I am someplace else —time out of mind—and the feeling persists for maybe two or three minutes. Sometimes I feel I am both here in this world and there in that world and that is a very strange feeling, let me tell you. Life with one foot in two doors.

None of the known causes of epilepsy are pretty: brain damage, brain infection, brain tumor, brain hemorrhage. I do not think there is anything wrong with my brain. My epilepsy is due to something else, some other abnormality, but I have no idea what. My seizures are often followed by drowsiness which lasts several hours.

During our courtship, I was forthright with Isabella. I told her my brain was filled with epileptic vibrations which could only be controlled and would never go away. I told her she could leave, that I would understand. In fact, that I *expected* her to leave. She said it did not matter. She would never leave. I loved Isabella for this. For her acceptance of my condition.

"Of course you know what this means?" I said. "It means I am not now and never will be normal. It means your life with me will be confusing at best. It means there will be good times and there will be bad. It means there will be times you will not know who I am. (There will be times *I* will not know who I am.) And still you can say that you love me?"

"Don't be silly," she laughed. "I love you for who *you* are."

* * *

The second moon I came upon was Ganymede, a pretty moon the color of milk chocolate. At 3,273 miles in diameter, it is the largest moon in the solar system, larger even than Mercury and Pluto and three-quarters the size of Mars. It would be a planet if it was in the right orbit only it isn't and that is really something to think about. Like Callisto, Ganymede is composed of a rocky core that takes up nearly half its diameter. It is covered with a thin crust of rock and ice. Its surface is a mixture of two types of terrain: old, heavily cratered regions, and younger regions with an extensive array of grooves and ridges. Visible in the north and south polar regions are bright polar caps, consisting of water frosts.

My destination was Crater Kittu, a dark crater about nineteen miles across. It took the better part of a day to reach Kittu from my spaceship and the skies were growing dark when I scrambled over the narrow rimwall and crossed the crater's smooth basin. It was in the middle of the basin, an area covered with volcanic deposits, where I found it: a stone image of Ganymede himself. The beautiful one. The statue was six feet high and exquisitely sculpted and if I had not known better I would have sworn it was alive. In his outstretched left hand Ganymede held a chalice.

I gaze at the statue and I sigh. It is so beautiful. I know that Isabella, like the statue, is immortal. In my mind she is immortal. I reach for the chalice. I know the liquid it contains will solve my problems. It will make me immortal. And then both Isabella and I will be immortal and we will never part. But of course the statue vanishes the moment my fingers are about to touch the magic cup. And I am left alone once again. Suddenly, I feel a seizure descending over me like a fog and I close my eyes and breathe deeply as the doctors had directed. Luckily the seizure passes quickly, but I am left alone and I am afraid.

✳ ✳ ✳

Isabella and I wed on the twentieth of October 1927, after a year-long engagement. (We would have wed immediately—so in love were we—but our parents insisted on the standard betrothal period.) The engagement was the happiest time of my life and as I think back on it now I can only weep at my good fortune. I don't believe I had a single seizure the entire time!

It was a wedding ceremony I will never forget. In attendance were Isabella's parents and mine. My two brothers. Her sister, her sister's husband, and their two children. And six of Isabella's friends.

"We are gathered here today . . ." the preacher began and that is all I remember. Isabella says I became rigid, my eyes staring into space, arms stiff at my sides. She says it lasted at least five minutes—longer than usual—and though she told everyone to remain calm they reached a point when they could wait no longer and a doctor was called.

I, of course, remember none of this. The next thing I recall Isabella and I were hand-in-hand, running down the church steps into a blizzard of rice. (Isabella told me later that just when the wedding party was about to panic, I snapped out of my trance and returned to normalcy. "I am not God," she said I said. Or rather whispered so that only she could hear.) She threw her bouquet into the air and her sister caught it. And I caught her eye—Isabella's eye—and I saw what I hoped I'd never see: a look of uncertainty. This only for a brief second, mind you, but one I would never forget. For, you see, though Isabella had always insisted she would never leave me—and though this most likely was true—she harbored lingering doubts. That look betrayed her.

* * *

My third destination was Io. A very interesting moon. Its surface is young and has almost no craters, unlike the others. It is the most active volcanic body in the solar system. Parts of its surface often change within weeks. Its terrain is mostly flat plains rising no more than a thousand feet though I have observed mountain ranges up to six miles high. The surface consists largely of sulfur with deposits of frozen sulfur dioxide. The surface itself is very colorful, mottled with red, yellow, white, orange, and black markings. Now, others may have their own favorites, but I think Io is the prettiest moon in the solar system. I wish I had married there. It is that beautiful!

I set my spaceship down near the moon's equator. I saw mountains and a variety of lava flows. A horseshoe-shaped lake filled with dark, basaltic lava. To my left loomed Haemus Montes, a rectangular-shaped mountain, and off in the distance Creidne Patera, a large, dark volcanic complex.

It was on the Maasaw Patera, one of Io's prominent mountain ranges, that I spied Princess Io. I called out to her but she did not respond. I had seen her several times before but had always been incognito—dressed once as a pastry chef, once as a diplomat, once as a priest—and I do not think she recognized me. There were several questions I wished to ask her, most notably: was it possible I was her son?

It is true Princess Io and I are separated in time by two thousand years. But it could be that I was her son then—as I am myself now—and that my epilepsy is the manifestation of my being both here in the now and there in the then. A simultaneity of sorts.

* * *

I have come to believe that my brain exists in two places at once and that the moons of Jupiter are the key. This, I tell Isabella, is why I must repeatedly return there. She does not understand and advises me to seek psychological counseling—insists on it, in fact—and says further that she will accompany me.

We spend many hours on a black leather couch in front of an elderly man with incandescent eyes. He has the odd habit of tapping his pencil on his desk before asking me a leading question and so I learn to anticipate the traps he is attempting to lure me into. Several times he wipes his brow with a handkerchief, as if he finds my mere presence unnerving, and his right foot swings back and forth like a metronome. His mannerisms become so bizarre I am certain he must be suffering from jungle madness. He listens to me and nods and occasionally says things that at the time seem to be of no consequence but in the end do seem to help. I conclude that perhaps I am mistaken. Perhaps my journeys to the moons of Jupiter are only flights of my imagination as the psychologist finally and triumphantly—with a thump of his fist on his pitted oak desk—claims.

$$* * *$$

Europa is the smallest of the Galilean moons, yet it is the sixth-largest moon in the solar system and is only slightly smaller than Earth's moon. It is the smoothest moon in the solar system and has only a few shallow craters. Europa's pale-yellow surface consists mostly of water ice; it looks like fractured glass that has been repaired by icy glue oozing up from below.

Europa is pulled in different directions by Jupiter and by the planet's other moons. The flexing of Europa's surface continues until the brittle crust cracks, causing volcanoes to erupt violently, showering the surface with material from below. This material forms Europa's most striking feature: dark streaks which crisscross the surface. Heat generated by the expansion and contraction melts part of the crust underneath the surface; this along with the infall of organic material from comets creates lakes that are filled with the building blocks of life.

There is a shallow crater in the southern hemisphere that is filled with liquid water. I scrambled over the rim of the crater—it's no more than several feet high—and came upon a scene of breathtaking beauty: an enormous lake perhaps one mile wide. The lake was dotted with islands that were composed of a darkish material. Blocks of ice, perhaps three dozen feet in diameter, floated on the surface. The air was deathly still. It was on the shores of this lake that I saw Europa of Agenor. She was a lovely creature, almost as lovely as Isabella. She was wearing a white robe and sandals. Her long blond hair was loose. She was looking out over the lake and did not hear me when I approached. I said nothing to her. I had no desire to startle her.

* * *

I remember when I told Isabella of my encounter with Europa and how she looked at me strangely. She took a deep breath and I saw that she was fighting back tears.

And it was then I realized I had lost her. I had lost Isabella.

She cried out angrily, "I never know when you're here or when you'll be away!"

I said simply, "I know."

She calmed down then and looked at me with her soft brown eyes. She started to sob. "I'm losing you."

"I'm always here," I said. "It's just that I'm not always *all* here."

"I can't live like this," she said. "No one could."

"But I love you."

"Love has nothing to do with it. You need help. Can't you see what's happening?"

I was silent.

"No," she continued. "I guess you can't."

What more could I say to Isabella? Only this: that many famous people were epileptics in their time: Julius Caesar, Vincent van Gogh, Fyodor Dostoyevsky, Peter the

Great, Charles Dickens, Isaac Newton, Sir Walter Scott, and Jonathan Swift.

And me, when I am not here and have gone to that other world. That world where immortality awaits.

But of course I said none of this. Instead, I begged forgiveness.

She looked away in fear.

And it was then that I played my final card. I suggested that Isabella come to Europa with me, to get away for a few days so we could rekindle our past love, but she would have none of it. "I can't do that!" she exclaimed, and for the first time in our marriage I began to wonder if perhaps every-thing was falling apart. It would have been nice to go with her, though, and who knows, maybe things would have turned out differently between us.

* * *

I no longer remember when I left Earth for the final time. I'd left so many times before, but had always returned, usually within a month, a week, a day perhaps, occasionally before I'd even left. "Isabella," I said the night before I van-ished into the cosmos forever. "Remember to call the re-pairman about our refrigerator; it's breaking down again." She smiled and kissed me on the cheek. There was nothing else to say.

* * *

It turned out that Isabella *did* call the repairman. He was there in the kitchen examining the refrigerator when I returned a week later to see how things were getting along without me. He didn't seem to notice me, at least he didn't acknowledge my presence when I walked into the room and said hello. He was a burly man, over six feet in height, with

21

thick brown hair and the ruddy face of a construction worker. He had pushed the refrigerator away from the wall and was examining the coils.

"They're shot," he said after a few minutes. "There's not a damn thing I can do."

Since I was not really present there was nothing I could say or do. Not that I would have said or done anything anyway. I stayed a few more moments, watching in wonder as they looked at each other like two people who had forgotten what it was that protocol demanded.

"The money," I whispered into Isabella's velvet ear.

She paid him and he thanked her. He wrote out a receipt and then he left. I stayed a moment longer, knowing the end was at hand, but finding it hard to leave. Sometimes even when you realize the time has come you find it impossible to say good-bye. Is-a-bel-la! If I could I would put you in my spaceship and fly off to the moons of Jupiter, for only on the moons of Jupiter is there nothing to fear and nothing for which one ever needs to be forgiven.

ALPHA CENTAURI

(February 16, 1928)

I t was just a short hop from there to the lovely binary star system of Alpha Centauri. I approached on a beam of light and was amazed by the grandeur of our galaxy: gaseous stars, compact stars, giant stars, stars giving birth to stars, stars spiraling into stars, blue planets, gold planets, blue and gold planets, planets shrouded in mist, naked planets, dark clouds of dust and debris. I came to rest on one of the many planets circling Alpha Centauri A and found it not unlike Earth, or rather, an Earth from long ago. I saw green fields and tall pine trees that swayed in a humid breeze. Gently rolling hills dotted with red and white wildflowers off in the distance. There were clouds in the sky but they were lime-green in color and translucent, unlike any I had seen before. The twin suns of the Alpha Centaurian system circled each other in a deadly embrace, their disks a golden hue. I recalled that this sector of the galaxy was home to dozens of binary star systems each hosting dozens of planets. The area should have been teeming with life.

Swarms of yellow butterflies rose before me. I followed them for nearly a mile over a winding dirt trail to a waterfall that overlooked a magnificent valley. I saw no creatures in the valley, nor signs that mammalian life had ever been present.

But—no!—I was mistaken. In the distance something *was* moving. I saw a dust cloud rising and a line of horses led by a woman on an Arabian stallion making their way towards a ring of fire. A holy caravan on its way to one of the pyramids of Ishtar. I shielded my eyes from the light of the blinding suns and the image vanished. It had been but an illusion. Or rather the memory of an illusion, for at that moment I realized this was an image from Earth's past, when the planet was young and teeming with life and death was an unknown word.

II

JASON AND THE ARGONAUTS

I had recently returned from the constellation Sagittarius and was unpacking my things, when Isabella brought the child to me.

"Franz," she said. "Where have you been?"

I took the child from my wife. I looked into his blue eyes. He smiled.

I asked Isabella how she was doing. She looked tired but that was understandable. I cursed myself for not being with her at the hospital; she must have hated me.

"I'm sorry," I said. "I was—"

"No," she said. "I understand."

As I looked at my child—my firstborn—the real world with its metallic claws retreated into the distance.

"The name?" I asked.

"The name we picked out: Jason. A lovely name, don't you think?"

* * *

Jason. Ah yes, Jason. My wandering son. Jason and the Argonauts. Jason and the Golden Fleece. I had taken Greek and Roman mythology in college and I fondly remembered the tale.

Jason—I recalled—was the son of King Aeson of Iolcus. The king had an evil brother, Pelias, who hated him. When Jason was only five, Pelias, in an act of madness, overthrew the king and imprisoned him in a dungeon many miles away.

Jason's mother—whom Pelias secretly desired—told Pelias that Jason had drowned himself in the sea out of grief. But what she really did was to send him far away to the land of Althira, where he was brought up by the centaur Chiron. She knew Pelias had plans to kill Jason and claim the throne of Iolcus for his own offspring.

King Pelias, as he was now known, was quite content. He had forced his brother's wife to marry him and he had everything he could desire, but even so he was always on his guard. He seemed to sense that others were plotting his death. The oracle told him he would rule over Iolcus until he was killed by a man wearing one sandal. When he heard this, King Pelias laughed and said, "I've never heard anything so absurd. Begone and never return!"

Several months later a young man with curly blond hair appeared in the marketplace. He was wearing a leopard's skin and only one sandal.

When King Pelias saw the stranger, he tried to remain calm. "What is your name?" he asked. "And why have you come to my kingdom?"

"My name is Jason," said the stranger. "I am the rightful king of Iolcus. My father is your brother, whom you have imprisoned."

"You are mistaken," King Pelias said. "Your father is not my prisoner. But, alas, he is no more. He died in battle while serving me. He was a brave and noble man. Do not fear—the throne shall be yours. But first you must bring me the Golden Fleece from the Kingdom of Colchis. It hangs on a tree there and is guarded by a dragon that never sleeps. It rightfully belongs to your kingdom. I have sent many men in search of it, but none have returned. I, as King, have failed miserably, for I promised your father I would recover it. But now you have arrived to lay claim as was foretold by the prophets of Iolcus. I am the luckiest man alive! I bless you on this glorious day!"

In truth, King Pelias knew Jason would never survive the journey and he would be rid of him forever.

* * *

When I was fifteen, I published a short story in a local literary journal. "Spaceflight" won first prize in the journal's annual competition and I was awarded five hundred dollars. My parents took the money (they said they would put it towards my college tuition), and it was the very next week that I began to experience the first symptoms of my disease: I had my initial out-of-body experience.

It wasn't epilepsy—not yet—but it was peculiar. I was walking down Hobart Avenue, daydreaming as I often did, when I—well, I was no longer *there*. In Peoria, Illinois. Physically I was there, taking up space on the sidewalk, but mentally I was someplace else. I saw nothing. I heard nothing. I felt nothing. I was enveloped in a cocoon of whiteness.

You might think I was terrified, but I wasn't scared at all! It was an interesting feeling, really. A calm and peaceful feeling.

I have no idea how long the experience lasted. But when I regained my senses, I hurried home. And now that I was myself once more, I realized I was trembling. "Mother," I said as I pushed through the front door. "I think I need to see a doctor."

* * *

As King Pelias thought things over, he became suspicious. "Your mother told me Jason killed himself," he said. "How do I know you are who you say you are?"

"I am he," Jason replied, "as my mother will attest. It was only a ruse to protect me. She thought you would kill me if you knew I was alive."

King Pelias laughed. "I would never entertain such a thought," he said.

Argus of Iolcus was a master shipbuilder and Jason's best friend. At Jason's request, he built a magnificent ship out of oak and pine. It was seventy feet long with sixty oars. The largest ship the Greeks had ever known. Jason put out a call for adventurers to help him capture the Golden Fleece. He signed up many great men. The ship was called the *Argo*, and the men, Argonauts.

On the first of September, they rowed away under a clear blue sky. Jason prayed to Zeus to bless the journey. The Argonauts pulled on their oars and sang songs of joy and the ship sped through the waves.

They had many adventures. One of the most notable involved the straights of Bosphorus which guarded the entrance to the Black Sea. The straits were filled with huge, floating rocks that moved together and had ripped apart many ships. The winds and the tides were so pronounced it was virtually impossible to safely pass through the waters. Jason was looking for a way around them when Amphiaraous, the wise man, said, "Let a dove fly through to show the way." Jason did so and observed the rocks smashing together behind the bird, but she made it through with only the loss of her tail feathers. "Forward!" Jason cried and the men of the *Argo* rowed with all their might as the rocks drew apart. Jason saw the rocks coming together again as the winds whipped from all directions. But they made it through without losing a single man. Only the rudder was crushed, which Argus repaired the next day.

* * *

"It might be epilepsy," the doctor said. "But then again it might not be. And even if it is, there is no reason to worry. Lots of famous people were epileptics." He reeled off a list of names, people I had never heard of.

Did I have any questions?

My mother was by my side. "Is there a chance Franz's condition will improve?" she asked.

Yes; in fact it was highly likely. As I matured, changes in my physical and mental makeup might well cause the epileptic symptoms to lessen. On the other hand, it was possible they could worsen. In fact, one could state the probabilities. In sixty percent of the cases the condition would eventually disappear. In thirty percent, it would become full-blown. In ten percent, it would remain the same.

At this point I stopped listening. I was dimly aware of my mother continuing to question the doctor and of him attempting to answer. I do not think he put her at ease for she was fidgeting with the hem of her dress, glancing at him uneasily, and then staring at the floor.

I wondered what all this meant. I might have epilepsy. I might not. I might improve. I might not. But one thing was certain: My mind worked in a different way. Of course I was scared. Who wouldn't be? But I was intrigued. Might not this realization prove to be the beginning of a long and noble journey?

Eventually the symptoms did go away. For a time.

* * *

The Argonauts rowed through the Black Sea for seven days. It was a peaceful time. They saw no one and amused themselves by telling tall tales. On the seventh day, they anchored at the port of Colchis, which lay at the eastern end of the sea. Colchis was a beautiful land, lush and green and covered with wildflowers. Jason said, "Here we will go ashore. The Golden Fleece lies in the middle of this land. It is guarded by a fierce dragon, whose fiery breath can incinerate any of us. Therefore, we must rest. Tomorrow's journey will be long and difficult and we may not survive."

Guided by a full moon, the Argonauts moved ashore. They set up camp a quarter of a mile inland and soon were fast asleep under the shining stars.

While this was going on, the goddesses Hera and Athena were watching from the heights of Mount Olympus. They had taken a liking to Jason and they asked Aphrodite, the goddess of love, to help him in his quest. "Aphrodite, dear," they said. "You must make the daughter of the king of Colchis fall in love with Jason. Indeed, it should not be hard. King Pelias has told King Aetes of Jason's mission. He said Jason will be asking for the Golden Fleece, but that what he really intends to do is to steal his daughter away from the kingdom. King Aetes plans a gruesome death for Jason and his crew. The king's daughter knows of her father's plans and is already troubled for she finds herself intrigued by stories of Jason's manliness. Her name is Medea. Only she can help the Argonauts with their mission."

* * *

"Yes," Isabella interjected. "I recall this part of the tale. But wasn't Medea really a butcher?"

"Yes, she was a butcher," I replied. "A butcher of human flesh."

Isabella shuddered. And for some reason I was reminded of a time—it seemed so long ago—when I shuddered in Isabella's presence. . . .

It was the year we met. Isabella was a part-time instructor at a dance academy in Las Cruces. She was talented, popular with the students, and the academy loved her. I was a junior at New Mexico State University. I had recently declared my major in astronomy and was attending a Friday afternoon departmental social when I saw her. Isabella. On the arm of a man. She took my breath away: her long, black hair, her dark-brown eyes, her immaculate complexion. When her boyfriend left to get something to eat, I took the opportunity to say hello. I looked into her eyes. And she looked into mine. I thought: I am in love. I felt a rush of adrenaline.

I told her I was majoring in astronomy, the study of the planets and the stars, that one day I would discover a major astronomical phenomenon and that I would name it after her, the most beautiful woman I had ever laid eyes on.

I took her hand and I closed my eyes. When I got the nerve to open them, I saw that she was smiling.

I never saw her boyfriend again.

* * *

King Aetes did not like Jason from the moment he set eyes on him. He asked Jason who he and his companions were and why they had come to his land. Jason replied, "I have come to ask you for the Golden Fleece. Whatever task you set before me, I shall perform in exchange for it."

The king wanted to strike Jason dead right then and there. How dare he lie to cover up his true intentions! Outside of Medea, the fleece was his most precious possession. And so he thought of an impossible task for Jason to perform. A task which would surely result in the man's death.

He said, "The Golden Fleece is yours. But first you must yoke to a plow two bulls that breathe fire. You must plow the fields on the outskirts of Colchis, and into the furrows of the earth you must sow the teeth of a dragon. These teeth are seeds from which a crop of armed men shall grow. They shall attack you and, without the aid of your companions, you must mow them down."

Jason was unmoved. "Tomorrow this shall be done," he replied. He wasn't sure how he would accomplish this task, but he knew that with the help of the Argonauts he could come up with a plan.

On Mount Olympus, Aphrodite instructed Mercury to fly down to Colchis and shoot an arrow of love into Medea's heart. When the arrow pierced her mortal flesh, Medea trembled and her eyes glazed over as the potion took effect. Later that evening, Medea sent one of her servants to bring Jason to her. She was trembling with lust; she could not sleep.

"Jason, my love," she said. "If you promise to take me as your wife, the Golden Fleece shall be yours."

Jason was thrilled. The Golden Fleece was soon to be his and Medea was exceptionally beautiful as well. He hugged her tightly and kissed her face and pearly neck. "Yes," he said. "It shall be so."

"Take this," Medea said as she handed him an ointment. "Spread it over your body. It will protect you from harm. And you will need this as well." She handed him twenty-four dragon teeth. Finally, she gave him a magic stone to throw at the armed men when they attacked.

The next morning Jason spread the magic ointment on his body and on his spear and his shield. Then he went to the field where King Aetes and his warriors awaited the spectacle.

"Jason is the dumbest man on the earth," said the king to his son Apsyrtus. "He will be torn limb from limb."

Jason strode out onto the field, and two fire-breathing bulls were set loose. At first it looked like it would be a quick kill as they thundered towards him. But Jason stood his ground, grabbed them both by the horns, and yoked them to the plow.

"The bulls breathe fire on Jason, yet they do not even singe him," Apsyrtus said. "How can this be?"

Of course he did not know about Medea's magic ointment.

"It doesn't matter," said the king. "Just wait until you see what happens in the next act."

Jason cracked his whip and the bulls dashed across the field. Into the furrows, he sowed the dragon's teeth. There was an explosion and an army of men sprang up and attacked him with a fury rarely seen in the kingdom. The king rose to his feet to better observe the killing, but suddenly Jason threw the magic stone into the army's midst. The men stopped and looked at each other in confusion. Then they began killing one another with their spears. Blood was everywhere. It flowed in and around Colchis like a river of death.

$$* * *$$

We left the party when the clock struck midnight. Holding up the key, I asked Isabella to accompany me to the university observatory.

"I love this place," I said as we entered the darkened tower. I opened the dome and we looked out onto a sky that was full of stars.

"Do you come here often?"

"Once or twice a week. I'm doing research on the spectral properties of Type A stars. It's basic research, nothing special. But my advisor thinks I might get a paper out of it." Then I changed the subject. "There's nothing like gazing into the heavens on a moonless night, Isabella. Don't you agree?"

She nodded.

"It's so peaceful."

"It is."

I looked away for a moment, then I turned back and looked into her eyes. I said, "I come here when I feel troubled."

"Yes," she replied. "There's nothing like gazing upon the cradle of existence to put life in perspective."

I was astounded. Without a doubt I had discovered a kindred spirit. And it was then that I decided to take a chance.

"Isabella," I said. "I can talk to you."

She looked puzzled.

"I mean, I can tell you how I feel." I shuffled my feet. "I belong up there. In the heavens. Among the planets and the stars."

"We all do," she said, without batting an eye. "It's where we came from and where we'll be again one day."

"You don't understand," I said. "I *go* there. Sometimes two or three times a week."

I looked up into a magnificent sky, at the belt of Orion that seemed to possess a supernatural glow. "You know—" I began.

Just then I felt Isabella's hand in mine. Nothing could have been more unexpected—or more welcome.

* * *

It wasn't long before all the men lay dead upon the ground. The king was beside himself with anger. "Jason is a scoundrel!" he cried and with his fists he beat the ground. "But he will not make a fool of me. Tonight—as per our agreement—he expects me to hand over the Golden Fleece. Well, I'll give it to him and let him return to his ship. But before he sets sail my men will board the vessel and kill them all."

Medea knew what her father intended, for she had overheard him scheming with Apsyrtus. Before nightfall she stole to Jason's ship where she found him telling stories in the captain's cabin. "Jason," she said, "you have little time left. There will be no Golden Fleece for you if you do not heed my words. My father plots your death and the death of your men. He is doing King Pelias' bidding. Come with me. I know where the Golden Fleece lies. I will take you there under cover of night."

Jason did not doubt her words. He always seemed to know when death was drawing near, and besides, the look in Medea's eyes convinced him she spoke the truth. Accompanied by her, he took a dozen of his men and rowed towards the shore. They followed the coastline for several miles. By now it was quite dark. The moon and stars were obscured by clouds. Medea cried suddenly, "Beach your rowboat here!"

"Jason and I will go alone," Medea said when they were safely on shore. "If we do not return by dawn, you will row back to the ship and leave this dreaded land."

The men began to protest—they could never leave their leader behind—but Jason ordered them to obey.

Jason followed Medea inland and eventually they came upon a forest of evergreen trees. "This way," she said as she entered the forest. They walked for what seemed like an eternity and eventually the forest was plunged into darkness. Truth be told, he was starting to question his decision to follow her when the forest opened into a magnificent grove. There, hanging from the limb of an oak tree, they saw the Golden Fleece. It was glistening in the light of a silvery moon that had emerged from behind the clouds. If only it would have been as simple as plucking it from the tree! Alas, a huge, fire-breathing dragon guarded the Golden Fleece. Jason had never seen such an enormous creature.

"Do not fear," he said to Medea. "The dragon will be no match for me."

Jason pulled out his sword and started towards the dreaded creature who reared back its head and prepared to strike him dead. What Jason did not know was that no man was a match for this dragon. But Medea knew what to do. She snuck up behind the dragon and sang a magical lullaby which lulled it to sleep. Jason pulled down the Golden Fleece. Then he stabbed the dragon seven times and watched as its blood flowed upon the earth.

He and Medea returned to the rowboat, where the men were overjoyed to see them. "We must hurry back to the ship," Jason said. "Death nips at our heels."

It was not until they were safely on board that Jason held up the Golden Fleece. The men marveled at the prize they had traveled so far to obtain. "It was all because of the lovely daughter of King Aetes," Jason said. "I would be dead if it hadn't been for her." Then he told them what had happened.

"But how will Medea get back to the palace?" the navigator Nauplius asked when Jason had finished. "Surely they realize by now that something is amiss."

"She's not going back," Jason replied. "Tomorrow Medea will become my wife."

* * *

It was a day I will never forget. The day we wed. Flocks of crows flew overhead, framing a cloudless sky. The air was cool and crisp. It was the 20th of October. Las Cruces was beautiful in the fall, a time known as the desert's spring, a season filled with explosions of sunflowers, purple sage, and yellow bird of paradise.

"Do you, Franz Herbert, take Isabella Rutherford to be your lawfully wedded wife?"

"I do."

"Do you, Isabella Rutherford, take Franz Herbert to be your lawfully wedded husband?"

"I do."

We kissed.

That evening we had dinner at the campus pizzeria, then went out to the countryside where we spread a blanket and gazed up into the starry night. She told me her dreams and I told her mine. I would take her to the farthest reaches of the galaxy, I said, and she laughed. But I was deadly serious.

* * *

King Aetes was enraged when he learned Jason had stolen the Golden Fleece. "This cannot be!" he exclaimed. "Poor boy"—this was the dragon's name—"would let no mortal slay him." The king's anger turned to hysteria when he was told that Medea had vanished. The Argonauts have sailed away with my lovely daughter, he thought in dismay.

"Quickly!" he cried. "There is no time to lose!" He told Apsyrtus to round up an army of a hundred men to overtake them. They set out several hours later in the fastest ship he commanded.

Now that he had the Golden Fleece, Jason let down his guard, which he never should have done. (He did not anticipate that Aetes would send an army to overtake him.) While the ship proceeded slowly through calm waters, he praised the men for their courage.

When Medea saw her father's ship approaching she had to think fast. She sent a message to her brother by a white dove. She had been kidnapped by Jason, she wrote, and had no desire to leave the kingdom. She told her brother she knew where Jason had placed the Golden Fleece. She would convince Jason to stop at a nearby island; the men were tired after their ordeal and needed a few days' rest. After securing the Golden Fleece, she would accompany the men ashore. When they were asleep she would meet Apsrytus and give him the fleece. Then they would kill Jason, slaughter the Argonauts, and return to their father.

Medea told Jason of her brother's plans and of her own scheme. He was awed by her ingenuity. They landed on an unknown island the very next day. When Apsyrtus arrived to recover the Golden Fleece, Jason was waiting for him: he sliced off his head with a single stroke of his sword and in unison the Argonauts raised their swords before Apsyrtus' terrified men. Medea's robe was covered with her brother's blood, but she was so cold-hearted she only laughed. "Death to the bastards of Colchis!" she cried.

Apsyrtus' army begged for mercy. "Prepare to die!" Medea said and she opened her arms as if in supplication to the gods above. She cast a spell upon the men and they slumped to the ground. Then Jason and his men slaughtered them like cattle. The next day they boarded the *Argo* and sped home. The ship's doctor, Asclepius, married Jason and Medea that evening as a gentle breeze blew. The crew roared their approval and all through the night they sang songs of joy. Jason smiled and he wrapped his arms around his bride.

Who is to say if Jason was truly in love or if Medea had cast a spell upon him? In a sense it didn't matter. The poor man had never known such happiness.

* * *

First years are wonderful. I obtained my bachelor's degree in physics and astronomy from New Mexico State University in 1928 and found employment at an aerospace company in Chicago. The work was challenging, but ultimately unsatisfactory, and when I was offered a position at

Lowell Observatory in Flagstaff, Arizona, I jumped at the opportunity. My first assignment was to track the movements of Venus and Mars. You might think it odd but I saw in the motion of those planetary bodies a dance not unlike that which occupied Isabella and me.

$* * *$

Jason pointed out the planets Venus and Mars, and Medea marveled at their beauty. He spotted a star going nova, a brilliant blue star in the constellation Cassiopeia. "Perhaps one day . . ." he sighed.

After a journey of several weeks the *Argo* landed at Iolcus. Crowds of people lined the dock for the ship had been spotted in the distance hours before. As the triumphant Argonauts debarked from their ship, Jason held the Golden Fleece above his head. The crowd roared and King Pelias was summoned. When Pelias saw Jason with the Golden Fleece and King Aetes' daughter at his side he pretended to be pleased.

What Jason didn't know was this: King Pelias had killed Jason's father the day the *Argo* had sailed and Jason's mother had thrown herself into the sea out of despair. When Jason's best friend Mopsus took him aside and told him the news Jason's heart was heavy with grief. He could not control himself and he put his head on Mopsus' shoulder and cried.

The next day Jason told his wife what had happened. At first she did not believe him, but Mopsus was able to convince her. Jason told Medea he would have to murder Pelias to avenge his parents' deaths. She was overjoyed at her husband's conviction. And she wanted to have some fun with the deed. She said, "I know what we must do. First, I will convince the king's daughters that I have discovered the secret of eternal youth. And then the trap will have been laid."

Medea went to King Pelias' home. There she told Pelias and his daughters that she had discovered the secret of eternal youth. Were they interested? Of course they were! They went out to a meadow on the edge of town. Medea slaughtered an old goat that was grazing in the meadow and boiled it in a cauldron she had brought there earlier in the day. She sprinkled the water with magic herbs. Moments later a young goat leaped out of the cauldron and scampered across the meadow. "See," she said. "It's easy."

The daughters were amazed. "You mean our father will be able to live forever?" the oldest one asked.

"Yes!" Medea replied, "and you, too." She cast a spell to put King Pelias to sleep. Then the daughters cut up their father and put him in the boiling water. This time Medea added nothing to the brew, and Pelias did not return to life. As the daughters recoiled in horror, Medea laughed and told them how vain they were.

Medea thought she had won Jason's love forever, but even this was not to be. As the years passed, he grew fearful of his evil wife and one day he fell in love with Arianna, a charming young girl from Corinth who was only seventeen.

Medea was enraged at Jason's behavior. She herself was nearly forty and was concerned that she no longer appealed to her husband. And her eyes nearly popped from their sockets when she learned that Jason and Arianna were to be wed. She tried to talk him out if it, but he would no longer even speak to her. On their wedding day, she sent Jason's bride a beautiful robe that she had sprinkled with poison. Jason knew at once that Medea intended some evil, but before he could utter a word, Arianna put it on. The robe burst into flames, killing her instantly.

The next day, while Jason was grieving, Medea strangled their two children. And as night was falling, she fled in her chariot drawn by dragons and was never heard from again. Jason was like a dead man: never again would he hear his children's voices and his beloved wife-to-be was dead. He had looked forward to the day when his children and his children's children would play together by the sea. Now this would never be. He would have killed himself had he the courage, but even that noble trait seemed to have abandoned him.

Jason's trials were not yet over. His home was struck by lightning the very next month and burned to the ground. He became a hermit and traveled from place to place. But he never said a word to anyone and the few people who did approach him came to regret it. In the end, he was ostracized. Ten years later, he returned home to gaze at the *Argo*—it had never sailed again—but no sooner had he done so than the rotting prow fell on his head and he died. He was fifty years old.

* * *

You ask what became of the Golden Fleece? One might expect a tragic end for Jason's most valued treasure, but its fate was far better. When Orpheus saw that Jason was no more, he swooped down from Mount Olympus, snatched up the Golden Fleece, and hung it in the temple of Zeus. It belonged to the mightiest of the gods, he said. It hangs there so that all of us can marvel at it and even now recall the remarkable feats of Jason and the Argonauts. You see, Isabella, the cycle of life is perpetual. Nothing dies, everything remains.

ARIEL

(October 14, 1929)

Venus is the goddess of love and Venus is the planet of love. When I slip beneath the clouds that shroud the second planet from our sun, I am both surprised and pleased to find a terrain covered with forests and vegetation—and overflowing with animal life. Surprised, since earlier observations indicated a barren world covered with mountains of molten lava. Pleased, since this means my stay will not be unpleasant.

The surface of Venus, as I behold it, consists of gently rolling plains that stretch to the horizon. The winds, which roared in the upper atmosphere, are a mere whisper at the surface. This is a lightly cratered world—meteors quickly burn up in the dense sulfuric atmosphere—and the nearby craters I see are both enormous and shallow. There are two highland areas: Ishtar Terra in the north and Aphrodite Terra in the south. Both are the size of large continents. There is also an enormous volcanic mountain range, Maxwell Montes.

In 1686 the Frenchman Bernard de Fontenelle wrote that the inhabitants of Venus were a small black race, burned by the sun, full of wit and fire, playing lutes with gay abandon, and always in love.

The nymphs, when I see them, are tall, white as snow, and reclusive. I see no signs of musical instruments, but they sing with a sweet, plaintive wail. They dart away when I emerge, their eyes wide with fright.

There is one maiden—I name her Ariel—who is not shy like the others. She gazes at me as if entranced. Most likely she is: I am her first human contact. She wears a white dress and sandals. Her complexion is rosy, her smile enticing. Her long blond hair falls to a thin waist. The beauty of her light-green eyes is intoxicating, and I call out her name as I draw near.

Alas, a fateful mistake! She has never heard a human voice—or those airy syllables Ar-i-el—and with a cry she turns and flees across the Venusian plain. I follow her for as long as I am able, but the distance between us slowly increases. I think she thinks it is a game, for several times she looks back and laughs.

Suddenly I realize it is growing hotter. I look around. Vegetation vanishes and the forests melt away into nothingness. The air, once light and fresh, is heavy and almost unbreathable. Nearby, volcanoes erupt, oozing lava into pancake-like puddles on endless stretches of craters and canyons and desiccated plains. I have deceived myself. Venus is a long-dead world and the fair Ariel nothing but an illusion.

Or perhaps not. Perhaps Ariel and her sister nymphs do exist, and I am but an illusion to them.

III

THE RINGS OF SATURN

Jason was three months old and his colic was raging. I remember picking him up from his crib at two in the morning, holding him against my chest, and patting his back. I would have to pace back and forth for a half hour or more, but it usually worked. Ah—but the trick was getting him to sleep, for as soon as I put him in his crib he started crying again and I would have to repeat the procedure. Sometimes it took an hour or two to get him in a sound slumber. It was exhausting. I took it all upon myself, though, for Isabella needed her sleep.

I took it all upon myself when I was home, that is. And that was the problem. The demands of my job kept me at the observatory most nights. My superiors had been so happy with my work on Venus and Mars that they assigned me a third project: to determine the existence or nonexistence of "Planet X," a planetary body rumored to lie beyond the orbit of Neptune. Percival Lowell had searched for it in vain for twenty-five years, but with the methods I was pioneering perhaps I could do better.

I explained this to Isabella one wintry December evening. If I was successful, I said, our life would surely improve. The money would be there, for one thing. And I assured her that my next assignment would allow us more time together.

She told me she intended to get a job before the year was out.

* * *

The first thing I did was give Planet X a name. (How can we discover things if they don't have names?) I called it "Pluto" after our faithful Persian cat. My calculations showed the region of the sky where it must lie—based on an unexplained wobble in the orbit of Uranus—and it was far out in the solar system, let me tell you!

* * *

Our solar system is divided into the inner—terrestrial—planets and the outer—gaseous—planets. But most of the solar system consists of empty space. Take a moment to consider: The inner planets are, in order: Mercury, Venus, Earth, and Mars. The outer planets are Jupiter, Saturn, Uranus, Neptune, and Pluto. The distances between the Sun and the inner planets are constant and relatively small. But this is not true with the outer planets. Saturn is twice as far from the Sun as Jupiter. Uranus is twice as far from the Sun as Saturn. Neptune is twice as far from the Sun as Uranus. (This is known as Bode's Law.) So I shall begin my search for the missing planet at twice the distance of Neptune to the Sun.

* * *

Unfortunately, Isabella was unable to find a job as satisfying as the one she had in Las Cruces. She ended up as a

46

teacher's assistant in a local pre-school. (I think she may have resented me for this, and it was, perhaps, the first sign of discord between us.)

My work at Lowell occupied not only the nighttime hours but much of the day as well; I was only able to care for Jason on Tuesday and Thursday mornings when Isabella was at work. This meant we rarely saw each other, and when we were together it was as if we were strangers.

Isabella: My feet are aching. Those kids never rest.

Franz: Let me tell you about Saturn. What a wild, crazy planet!

Isabella: The kids are wild and crazy. Some days I wonder if this is really the job for me.

Franz: From far away Saturn is beautiful, but when you're on the planet, it's simply indescribable.

As I look back I see what a horrible situation it was. It led us to grow apart, though the effects were not fully felt until years later.

$$* * *$$

Jason was a wonderful child. Now nearly a year old, he had begun to take his first tentative steps. Often he would stumble and fall, but he was quick to pick himself up and start again. At times he would look back at me and smile as if to say, "See if I care!"

$$* * *$$

After Jupiter came Saturn with its magnificent rings.

The trip to the sixth planet from the Sun was uneventful, but it was always interesting. The space between Jupiter and Saturn is filled with a gelatinous substance which makes travel slow. And yet the space I inhabit seems to go on forever. A black, inky smoothness that expands in all directions.

I traveled for a long time through that inky void. And in the end I realized I was lost in space. You shouldn't have left home, Franz, I thought. A pointless statement to be sure, for I *had* left home. With nothing else to do I screamed, or rather I tried to do so, but it was a pathetic attempt, a voiceless cry, for sounds do not carry in the vacuum of space.

* * *

Sleep. Sleep. Isabella needed sleep. The demands of motherhood were exhausting. And it didn't help that I was away nearly all the time. Did I feel guilty? You bet! But it wasn't as if I could do anything about it. My epileptic mind controlled me at this point. Epilepsy is like that. You think you have it under control, but it really controls you.

"Isabella, my darling. Is there anything I can do before I leave?"

"No, Franz. Please. Stay a few minutes longer."

"I shan't be long, I promise. But Saturn beckons. Saturn with its magnificent rings."

* * *

Saturn is the most beautiful planet in the solar system. It has an atmosphere that resembles butterscotch and a ring system—ah!—a ring system that is the envy of the cosmos. It extends 180,000 miles from the planet—about the same distance as from the earth to the Moon!

There are three main rings, the A, B, and C rings, each only a half-dozen feet in thickness. The rings themselves are made up of many smaller rings called ringlets. The ringlets are composed of ice particles that range in size from snowflakes to small boulders. Several of Saturn's smaller moons orbit within the ring system and help to form the rings into braided strands. These moons are called shepherds. Two of them are named Prometheus and Pandora.

* * *

I am supposed to be examining the orbits of Venus and Mars as well as searching for a phantom planet. And then there is a third assignment: to determine the chemical composition of Jupiter's moon Europa. But in truth all this bores me. (I found Pluto the other day, by the way, but I didn't tell anyone. It is an iceball at the edge of the solar system. It shall be my secret.) I would prefer to look farther away, at distant galaxies, nebulae, and quasars. If my superiors at Lowell knew what I was doing I would be fired, but I don't care. I'm not sure what it is, really. This desire that consumes me. I need to know where I came from. My ancestry.

My grandfather was made in one of those stars. One of the stars in the Sombrero Galaxy. My grandmother heralds from deep within the Andromeda Galaxy, a place I have never been to but where I will go before I die. Even more distant ancestors herald from places farther away, the quasars that lie at the farthest reaches of the cosmos. My own parents came from much nearer. From within our own Milky Way. Two stars I look upon often: Castor and Pollux.

* * *

I returned to an empty house, and instantly felt a wave of panic sweep over me. Isabella had taken Jason and left.

Isabella! Jason! I cried.

I searched the house. Perhaps Isabella had left a note? In the kitchen I saw dirty dishes in the sink. In the bedrooms two beds unmade. Dirty clothes littering the floor. A grocery list on the dining room table.

In the living room I lay down on the couch to wait. I stared at the wall, my mind blank. As blank and empty as the surface of a long-dead planet. Pluto hopped onto the couch and rubbed his head against my thigh, purring. I stroked his back. "Pluto, Pluto," I said. "Where is my wife? Where is Isabella?"

I wished I was stroking Isabella's back. I love her so much it hurts. She who is composed of light and air.

* * *

Saturn is the only planet less dense than water. In the unlikely event that a large enough lake could be found, Saturn would float in it. Saturn is classified as a gas planet: it doesn't have a surface. It is composed of seventy-five percent hydrogen and twenty-five percent helium. It seems that the heavier elements fell into the inner solar system as it was forming and created Mercury, Venus, Earth, and Mars. The outer planets (except for Pluto) are gaseous. Saturn has ferocious winds, five times as powerful as the greatest hurricanes on Earth. They blow mostly in an easterly direction and are strongest at the equator, lessening a bit at higher latitudes.

Heedless of the tragic end that might await me, I descend. The winds are so fierce I fear my limbs will be torn away. My mind freezes. There is a roar in my ears. I hear only the howling winds. I shout but my voice is lost to the winds.

* * *

Imagine my amazement when the back door opened and Isabella and Jason came into the house. I jumped up and rushed to greet them. "Daddy," Jason crooned. "Dad-dy."

"Where were you?" I asked. I must have sounded judgmental for Isabella replied somewhat harshly:

"I didn't bother leaving a note, Franz. I never know when you'll be back."

"I'm sorry," I said. "I was worried."

I went into the bedroom and laid down on the bed and soon was fast sleep.

I had a dream.

I am Albert Einstein presenting a paper on the Special Theory of Relativity at the Seventh International Conference on Astrophysics. I am greeted skeptically and this surprises me. Afterwards several prominent physicists come up to me and express their doubts. No one knows, they say. No one knows, no one knows, no one knows.

I know.

You, sir, are a strange man.

I am Albert Einstein. I know many things and have been to many places.

Your analysis makes no sense. It runs counter to everything we believe.

What you believe may be wrong.

What we believe we believe to be correct.

Nevertheless, it may be wrong.

How exasperating!

Oh, don't you see? To err is human, to dream divine. What I believe may be wrong, but what you believe may be wrong as well and I have proved it with these equations. The universe is an equation. No physical object can travel faster than the speed of light, but the human mind can and often does.

* * *

Amazing! It turns out that Saturn has a surface, after all. (The reports obtained from telescopic observation at Lowell were wrong.) I open my parachute and, buffeted hither and thither, descend to the surface. I land gently, for the ground is as soft as a marshmallow. What a surprise: a marshmallow planet! The winds that swirled with unimaginable ferocity in the atmosphere, are nonexistent here.

I look around. It is white. As far as the eye can see. It is a whiteness that blinds. There are no discernible features on the surface of this planet. Not a crevice or a crack. I've never seen anything like it. An empty canvas. I walk for maybe an hour, but the scene never changes. For all I know I went round in circles and am back where I started. Wouldn't that be strange!

* * *

And then there was the time I convinced myself I was Vincent Van Gogh. That was really something. Franz Herbert. Master Painter. My medium was oil. Surrealistic paintings of the cosmos: galaxies, nebulae, planets, and stars. I would stare at my masterpieces for hours on end. It was probably the many colors of Saturn's atmosphere that caused me to take up painting. I had never seen so much color as when I was descending to the surface, the winds whipping around me. It was terrifying. I thought: If I survive and return to Earth, I shall take up painting and I shall paint a picture of Isabella.

* * *

I take out my shovel and begin to dig through the Saturn's mushy mantle. When I break through the crusty outer layer (which is perhaps three feet thick) I find the inside to be gooey and moist. The going is easier now. My shovel sings. After several hours I reach the rocky core at the planet's center. It's the size of a large boulder on Earth and glows molten-red like a fire engine's beacon. I remember that Saturn generates more heat than it receives from the Sun. Now I know why.

There is no way I can penetrate that rocky core so I do the next best thing: I go around it.

"Hi-ho, hi-ho, it's off to work I go!" I sing as I tunnel back up to Saturn's surface. I see the rings of Saturn once again, as beautiful as ever, and beyond them (far, far beyond) Uranus, Neptune—and Pluto.

$$* * *$$

I was staring at a picture of Pluto when Isabella came upon me. It must have been the way I was looking at the planet—as if I were in a trance—for she uttered a cry. I was so far gone I didn't even look up.

"Franz?"

"Don't bother me."

"Honey . . ."

"Leave me alone."

"But—"

"I'm okay."

But of course I wasn't okay.

Isabella said nothing more, but neither did she leave. She wanted to help me, but she didn't know what to do.

"I must go there, Isabella," I said. "To Pluto. I must touch the surface of the planet. Do you know what it means to me?"

"Franz! No!" She was crying.

"No, no, no, Isabella. It will be fine. To touch the planet of the Underworld. It is beyond Saturn, of course. And Uranus and Neptune. And it has a solid surface. On which one can stand and view the Sun and the other planets of our solar system. As if one were on top of the tallest mountain peak. It is my world. My world, Isabella."

I turned away from the picture and looked at my wife. Her head was in her hands.

I sighed.

"Of course I won't go," I said. "I was only dreaming. Don't worry."

"Franz, you need to see the doctor."

What could I say? I've seen the doctor and he's a silly man. He speaks of my epileptic mind, but he has no idea what I'm going through. I am composed of subatomic particles that wink in and out of existence. I am oblivious to reality much of the time. I don't know why Isabella didn't leave me long ago. She must love me more than I ever imagined. More than I deserve. I am a half-husband.

"I'll call in the morning," I said. "I think my medication needs to be adjusted."

MERCURY

(December 17, 1929)

Because the surface of Mercury is as hot as molten lead, its inhabitants live underground. It has an atmosphere, though, and properly suited up one can live on the surface for brief periods of time.

The planet is heavily cratered, much like Earth's moon. It has cliffs the color of ochre that extend as much as a mile into the sky. Evidence of ancient lava flows are everywhere. There are shallow basins and ringed craters. A good percentage of Mercury's surface is covered by plains.

Mercury has its oddities, as well. And they are bizarre! I observe the Sun setting in the west, a small red disk. And then—almost immediately—it rises and increases in size as it reverses course. At its zenith it stops and changes direction, growing smaller until it disappears from view. The stars come out and speed across the sky at three times their normal rate. I spy Earth, a small, pale-blue disk about the size of my thumb. I feel sad that it is no longer my home, this third planet from the Sun.

Eventually, I find what I am looking for: one of the many entrance holes that lead underground. This one is nearly four feet wide, partially obscured by fallen rock. It is built into the side of a cliff fronted by windswept blue-grey boulders. I noticed it only because I thought I saw something moving amongst the rocks.

The entrance is surrounded by yellow vegetation and tall stalks made of a material that looks like petrified wood. I see a swift-moving stream of boiling water that flows beyond the entrance, and I watch in fascination as steam rises, condenses against the cliff wall, and trickles to the ground.

From out of nowhere the brown body of a Mercurian rat shoots across my path and disappears into the hole. I jump back, startled. I thought Mercury was too hot for anything to live on the surface. Or was this animal but an illusion?

I enter and find myself in a maze of tunnels. Everywhere I look there are veins of gold, diamond, sapphire. A miner's paradise!

The tunnel is suffused with light which glows red like the embers of a dying fire. Try as I might, I cannot discern the source.

I walk on through damp, serpentine passages. I hear the drip, drip of water falling over polished rocks. More than once I slip, scattering stones in all directions. The tunnel opens and I am walking along a ridge, the escarpment of an underground cliff. I watch my step lest I plunge to what surely would be a gruesome death. (I imagine myself as a bloodied corpse, a prisoner down here forever.) Eventually, though, the tunnel walls close in and I breathe a sigh of relief.

An hour later I find myself a mile below the surface. The passage ends and I am facing a melancholy landscape with no sign of life. The soil has a bluish hue and is compact like hardened clay. The air is cool, still, and deathly silent. If I lived down here I surely would go mad!

I notice six passageways and pick one at random. I walk for another mile or so but encounter nothing. The passage descends, narrows, and I am conscious of thick, musky air pressing down upon me. My lungs feel as if they are about to burst. My heart pounds, I am sweating about my neck and forehead. And then everything goes black.

I must have fainted, for the next thing I know I am lying on my back. The pressure on my chest is overwhelming. I gasp for breath.

Perhaps I've miscalculated and I am closer to Mercury's core than I'd imagined? To be honest, it's possible I've been walking for days, not hours. I've lost all sense of time.

With a Herculean effort I rise and start off once again. How to describe what I see?—or more precisely, what I think I see, for the light in the tunnel is virtually nonexistent.

I detect amorphous shapes which hover before me with appendages like the talons of a hawk. They want to claw out my eyes, I know. There are ghosts down here. I see shadows of forms that once were, grinning, toothless faces. I feel fiery breaths. I raise my arms—a pathetic shield—and scream in terror. Yet the ghosts, too, must be afraid for they scurry into the shadows.

No, I will not find an inhabitant of Mercury today and probably never will. It is far more likely that I have descended into the underworld and now am walking among the skeletons of the damned.

IV

THE BLACK HOLE

I found Pluto as I said, and, as I said, I didn't tell a soul. For, as I said, it would be my secret. At least for a while.

Luckily, it didn't matter. I had other projects going, one of which catapulted me onto center stage. Right then. When I needed a distraction.

I became famous in the spring of 1930 for my work in detecting the first black hole. That such an object had been discovered did not come as a surprise to the scientific community, which had been aware of the theoretical possibility for some time, but that the black hole was found orbiting a planet and that the planet was Earth did raise eyebrows.

I was in the kitchen cooking dinner when without warning a cast-iron pot rose from the stove, hovered in mid-air for several moments, as if unsure of what to do with its newfound freedom, then disappeared out an open window, leaving only wisps of steam behind. I knew what this meant—my research had been leading me in this direction for some time—and my hands began to tremble. I called out to Isabella but she did not answer. Then I remembered she had taken Jason and gone shopping several hours before.

The news was so important it had to be delivered in person. I rushed over to the observatory and burst into my boss' office. This was confirmation of the research I had painstakingly conducted over the past several years, I said. Research he had not known about because I hid it from him.

"You what?"

"I didn't think you would approve."

"They've been saying this about you for some time, Franz," he said. "They have been saying you're nuts."

"Maybe," I said, "but think of what this means to humanity."

"The idea is preposterous."

"Hardly," I insisted. I had to press my case. "It means time travel is possible. You go into the black hole and you come out somewhere else in the cosmos. The only problem is how you return, but further research should—"

"If," he began, stabbing the air with his index finger, "if black holes exist—which I seriously doubt—and if one were to be found orbiting the earth, why, we would all be sucked inside and torn to shreds! In the wink of an eye. Now I ask you: have we been torn to shreds? No. The very fact that we are in a room having this absurd conversation proves that no black anything is orbiting the earth."

∗ ∗ ∗

A black hole is an object whose gravity is so strong not even light can escape from it. Just as the earth is strong enough to pull an object such as an apple back to its surface, a black hole bends light around its core. Black holes form from the remnants of exploded stars. With nothing to oppose gravity, the remnant collapses upon itself. It becomes a point of infinite density known as a singularity. I think of the singularity as a many-eyed monster with a mouth that is agape. If you are unlucky enough to find your way inside, you quickly disappear into the belly of the beast!

Finding a black hole is not an easy task. Since light cannot leave its surface, it follows that the object cannot be seen. One must rely on indirect means. For months I had been combing the universe looking for regions of space where black holes might lurk. I had been unsuccessful. Several areas looked promising—including one at the center of our own galaxy—but I could confirm nothing. Indeed, there always seemed to be another explanation. I asked Isabella if she thought I should give up—success would never come my way, I lamented—but she insisted I continue my search. "You are only twenty-four," she said. "At the start of your career. Rest assured that one day you will find what you are looking for."

* * *

My boss had spoken too soon. Within days objects from all over the country were being sucked up into the atmosphere. A ladder from Cincinnati. A dump truck from Boston. A child's swing set from Pittsburgh. A supermarket from Seattle. The entire town of Decatur, Illinois.

The houses of Congress were in an uproar. Was this a new weapon of war? The unfolding of an enemy plot? Most certainly, the doomsayers said, and not only did it signal the end of our country but also the end of the world. They laid out the steps of the coming destruction: first America would be ripped out of the earth and devoured whole—first, for it had been first in everything; then Europe for its refusal to stem the tides of its outrageous excess; third, Africa, simply for being where it was; and finally the entire continent of Asia which had done nothing for eternity but pray to false gods. Only the polar continents would be spared and those simply because the Creator knew they had never sinned.

* * *

I determined that the radius of the black hole orbiting Earth was two miles—a black hole this size had the same mass as the Sun, I told my associates at Lowell. This news sent hearts palpitating throughout the observatory—had our Sun—the sustainer of life—been transformed into a cosmic vacuum cleaner? But when the next day arrived, and the rays of dawn shown from the East as they always did, it became clear that it was not so.

And since it was not so, where had the black hole come from? No one had the answer. I scratched my head in puzzlement, for I could not understand why a black hole would form in a region of space known to exhibit such extreme negativity. And by that I mean negativity in a positive sense. The negativity of the planets that kept our solar system orderly. One would have thought that the black hole— the antithesis of order— would perish in the tidy environment which was the solar system.

I named the black hole Pluto Redux. Why it had formed in this section of the galaxy was unknown and perhaps unknowable, but that it was there and that it was consuming the earth was undeniable. By my calculations it would finish digesting America within a week and then would turn its attention to Europe. The entire planet had perhaps a month left.

* * *

"He is mad."
"As mad as can be."
"Shall we dismiss him from the observatory?"

"Perhaps we should keep him awhile longer. He came highly recommended."

"And his work on Venus and Mars was first-rate."

"True. But this black hole nonsense. This time he has gone too far."

"He seems to lose his concentration often."

"I have observed him babbling like a child."

"The ramblings of a simpleton."

"Of a nutcase."

"Of a kook."

"Yes—but there is something to what he says. A kernel of truth, perhaps?"

"No—no truth. Only madness."

"Still. One never knows."

"It is sad. He has a wife and a young son."

"So sad."

"So sad."

"So sad."

But it is not sad at all. It is revelatory!

* * *

How would you experience a fall into a black hole? If you stayed outside the spherical surface that marks the boundary of the black hole—known as the event horizon—you would be just fine, for a black hole's gravity is no stronger than any other object of the same mass. If you orbited such an object and managed to keep your distance, you would be very cold and surrounded by darkness—you would undoubtedly want a lantern and a thick winter coat —but otherwise your life would not change.

But what if—wanderer that you are—you crossed the event horizon and began that fateful plunge towards the center of the hole? At first, you wouldn't feel any gravitational forces. Since you were in free-fall, you would be weightless. You might shout with joy at your newfound freedom. But as you got closer to the center these forces would get more intense. And at the center—shudder!—lies the unspeakable. What I have termed a singularity. It is the place where physical laws break down, where matter is crushed to nothingness by the infinite power of gravity, where space and time become meaningless.

What would you see as you were falling in? Surprisingly, you wouldn't see anything particularly interesting. Images of faraway objects might be distorted in strange ways, since the black hole's gravity bends light, but that's about it. Nothing special happens the moment you cross the event horizon. Even after you crossed it, you could still see objects outside, as light could still reach you. No one on the outside could see you, of course, since the light reflecting off you couldn't escape. I think of a black hole as a one-way mirror that reflects the cosmos.

Here is something interesting: *when you cross the event horizon distance and time switch roles.* Distance becomes a time-like phenomenon and time a space-like one. This means you can't stop moving forward in space just as previously you could not stop moving forward through time. It may sound strange but it is true: trying to avoid the center of a black hole is like trying to avoid tomorrow. It simply can't be done!

In your remaining seconds, you might panic and thrash about in a desperate attempt to avoid the singularity. Unfortunately, it would be hopeless, since the singularity lies in your future, and there is no way to avoid your future. In fact, the harder you thrash, the sooner you hit the singularity. It's probably better that way, though, for the death which awaits you is not pleasant. Better to get it over with at once.

* * *

It was decided that a space probe would be sent into the black hole. And that was where I came in. I had extensive experience traveling through the cosmos and was therefore a natural for the job. Outfitted in my spacesuit I climbed into my spaceship and blasted off. As I cruised through the blackness of space, I wasn't sure what fate awaited me, or even if I would recognize my end were it suddenly to arrive: if the black hole were to engulf me, would it be like drowning in emptiness or coming face-to-face with all that ever was?

* * *

Now you are not going to want to hear this but the situation is about to get even more confusing. Isabella is in her bedroom in Las Cruces looking out at the night sky. She watches as Franz nears the black hole. What does she see? Does she observe her lover being ripped to shreds as he plunges to the center? Even if Franz were to enter the black hole (which he will be careful not to do) she would not see this. Remember, if Franz were to cross the event horizon the light reflecting off him would no longer escape and she would be spared witnessing his horrible end. In fact, Isabella would never actually see Franz enter the black hole. As he got closer and closer to the horizon the light reflecting off him would take longer and longer to reach her. From her point of view he would be slowing down. The last photons of light would take an infinitely long time to reach her. He would seem to have come to a dead stop. Actually, he would have been torn apart by the colossal forces at the black hole's center but Isabella would never know this.

* * *

I realized I was approaching the event horizon when I detected a subtle change in the fabric of space; I cut my thrusters to avoid getting too close. Then I fired the probe into the hole just as I had been instructed by the space agency. Initially, the data I received was sporadic and confusing. It seemed to indicate that the probe was collapsing into an infinitely dense mass. Moments later I received a burst of data that was off the scale and then nothing. The probe had reached the singularity and perished. I listened awhile longer but to no avail. Silence can be dreadful.

Next, I fed the hole a steady stream of metallic objects, plasma, and X radiation. The hope was that if this could be done for a sufficient period of time the hole might become satiated and move off. I radioed Earth on a special wavelength that even the black hole did not know about and told them the news. Was there a diminishment in the hole's appetite? Unfortunately the reverse seemed to be the case: the scientists radioed back that the destruction on Earth was more horrendous than ever. It was as if the black hole became hungrier the more it consumed. I realized there was nothing I could do to quell the disturbance and so I prepared for my return journey.

* * *

The conclusion was inevitable: the black hole would end up consuming Earth. But then one day the black hole evaporated and I realized what had happened. It probably makes no sense to you but it is a natural consequence of the laws of physics. You see, black holes are not really black. They are more like a dull gray. And they emit radiation that causes them to shrink over time. Before you call me mad let me explain. According to physics matter can appear out of nowhere, but only if it disappears quickly. In the case of a black hole what happens is this: every now and then a particle and its opposite appear out of the vacuum of space with the particle coming into existence outside the event horizon and its opposite coming into existence inside the horizon. They are separated from birth, so to speak. The particle outside the horizon is emitted back into space, while its opposite is swallowed up by the singularity. This happens repeatedly, resulting in a steady stream of radiation from the black hole causing the hole to shrink and eventually disappear.

In the case of our black hole—the hole orbiting Earth—when this evaporation was complete the objects that had been sucked inside were freely emitted and descended on the earth with a blinding fury. It was known as the day of blinding light. Everyone on Earth was blinded on that day.

* * *

I have named it Pluto, I told my associates at Lowell. It is the ninth planet in the solar system. A small, rocky world about the size of Earth's moon. Those who had searched for it before me did not notice the planet, because it is about as conspicuous as a black hole. The day was February 18, 1930. A day that shall live forever.

But Pluto is not really a planet. It doesn't belong and that is why I have claimed it as my own. For I don't belong either. Not on this Earth.

But I do belong with Isabella. Even when I am dead and gone and memory fades.

The physicists were wrong. Black holes never really vanish. Nor will I, nor will Isabella, nor will our love which like an eternity is everlasting.

HOAG'S OBJECT

(April 2, 1930)

Nothing is more violent than when two galaxies collide. One destroys the other and it is not a pretty sight. Usually the vanquished galaxy is annihilated. Sometimes it is transformed into a galaxy of unusual shape —a donkey, a bird, a goat—and is flung far from its intended path. But the most interesting collision is not even a collision. It occurs when one galaxy passes close to a second and is ripped apart by gravitational forces. The remnants of the first galaxy are captured by the second and form a ring around it. The resulting structure is called a ring galaxy. They are rare cosmological entities, only a half-dozen are known to exist.

About 600 million light-years away in the constellation Serpens lies Hoag's Object, a ring of hot blue stars that circles a nucleus of aging yellow stars. This ring galaxy is about 120,000 light-years in diameter, slightly larger than our own Milky Way. It formed two billion years ago when a young galaxy passed too close to an older one. The former was shredded into what amounts to a smoke ring in the heavens, circling its predator. It will eventually collapse upon the latter, but that will not happen for another billion years. The gap between the blue ring and the yellow core is completely dark. I have spent time there and it is an experience unlike any other. Above you lies the fading blue light of the ring, below the fiery yellow core. You are between Heaven and Hell. You yearn for the one, but the other fascinates as well.

I have made an amazing discovery. In the dark gap of Hoag's Object lies a *second* ring galaxy. A miniature ring. And within the gap of this galaxy lies a third ring galaxy and within its gap a fourth and so on. Each is an order of magnitude smaller than the previous. I hop from galaxy to galaxy for as long as I am able. Until they become smaller than my own self and I am reduced to a mere spectator. I watch as they fade into the distance, until they become indistinguishable from a point. A mathematician's point. At the end of every event, imagination takes over and this was no exception. Every point contains within itself a ring galaxy. My mind is an infinitude of points comprising the space that I inhabit. It is a ring galaxy.

V

MANY HAPPY RETURNS

Fame came quickly then. Fame that I did not want. Or need.

"It's part of the game," my boss told me. "You've got to play it."

And play it I did. Wherever I went I had them eating out of my hand. Everyone wanted to see the man who discovered the ninth planet of the solar system. Everyone wanted to hear what he had to say. About life. About death. About the afterlife. Not that I was qualified to speak on any of those subjects. But they wanted me to. Night after night they begged for my insights into every problem known to mankind. It was as if they thought I was a prophet.

And so—by degrees—I gave them what they asked for. And why not? If they thought I was a prophet, why, a prophet I would be!

I wooed them in Albuquerque with my ruminations on man's place in the cosmos. I astounded them in Galveston with an in-depth analysis of the astronomer Galileo Galilei. In Charleston—where I was pressed to foretell man's destiny—I predicted that not only would mankind colonize the outer planets but that Pluto would serve as his outpost to the stars. And in New Haven, I delivered what came to be known as my "Sermon on the Mount":

Blessed are the poor in spirit, for theirs is the kingdom of heaven.

Blessed are they who mourn, for they will be comforted.

Blessed are the meek, for they will inherit the land.

Blessed are they who hunger and thirst for righteousness, for they will be satisfied.

Blessed are the merciful, for they will be shown mercy.

Blessed are the clean of heart, for they will see God.

Blessed are the peacemakers, for they will be called the children of God.

Blessed are they who are persecuted for the sake of righteousness, for theirs is the kingdom of heaven.

They went wild.

Staring out into a sea of adoring eyes. How many days and nights did I face them? And always those questions. Those endless questions. How I hated the questions:

Q: What was it like on those long, cold nights patiently searching the heavens?

A: Well, it's not what you might expect. I was so involved in the search I wasn't bothered by the long hours or the temperature. It's like that whenever you're searching for something you hold dear.

Q: Did you ever think you would fail?

A: Absolutely! In fact, I expected to fail. So many before me had searched for the elusive ninth planet and had come up empty. Why should I—a junior astronomer—prove to be any different?

Q: Has it been difficult for you to handle fame?

A: No, for the simple reason that I don't consider myself famous. I was simply in the right place at the right time.

Q: You look tired. Are you happy?

A: It's been a long day. But I've never been happier!

And always Isabella was by my side. To comfort me. To console me. To bring me back to Earth. But was *she* happy?

* * *

Five rivers surround Hades. The river Styx is the best known and the most sacred; it serves as a crossroads where the world of the living meets the world of the dead, where the world of the mortal meets the world of the immortal. It is coupled with the rivers Cocytus and Pyriphlegethon, which flow into the river Acheron, and the river Lethe which makes newcomers to the underworld forget their former lives. The rivers are so foul that to drink their waters causes instant annihilation. They bubble with fire.

There are many famous inhabitants of Hades. And many punishments as well. There is Cerberus, the three-headed dog who guards the entrance to Tartarus where the worst people are sent. Sisyphus, who is forever condemned to push a boulder uphill. Tantalus, who stands in a pool of water with fruit all around him yet can never quench his thirst or hunger. Aescelon, who is tied to a wheel of fire. Ithitus, who is forever struck by thunderbolts.

Sooner or later, all mortals came to Hades. Led by Hermes, the fleet-footed messenger of the gods, a dead person finds himself at the banks of the river Styx. Those who are buried properly find a coin under their tongue, which they present to Charon the ferryman. Charon is known for being quiet, and he ferries his clients across the river without saying a word.

Those who are not buried with a coin are doomed to wander the river's edge until they find the pauper's entrance to Hades, though there were exceptions. When Heracles went to Hades to bring back Cerberus on his tenth labor, he gave Charon such a menacing glance, that the ferryman took him across without payment. Odysseus, Aeneas, Orpheus, and Theseus were the only other living persons who ventured to Hades. All returned with horrid tales of the hideous scenes they had witnessed.

* * *

It was when we were in Chicago that I posed the question. I had just delivered a lecture to a group of academics from the University of Chicago. The applause was echoing in my ears while Isabella and I sat at an outdoor café on the waterfront, sipping lemonades.

"Are you happy?" I asked her.

She did not reply right away and I was pretty sure I had my answer.

"I don't know," she said finally. "I guess the lecture circuit doesn't suit me. I'd rather be home in Arizona."

"Me, too," I said and I took her hand. "But we must press on. It's for the good of the observatory, you know. They asked me to do this tour—they said the money coming in will fund half a dozen important projects—and I could hardly say no. It will be over soon."

"I keep telling myself that, but it just seems to drag on."

"I know."

"And . . ."

There was something else.

"Franz, I think all this may be going to your head."

I looked into her glassy eyes. I couldn't tell if she was serious.

"No, no," I said. "Though I see how you might feel that way. It's the crazy questions they keep asking me. They want me to be something I'm not. Some kind of a god. So I humor them."

"I don't think that's what they want. They want to know how you discovered Pluto, that's all. It's a fascinating story. You can't blame them for wanting to hear it."

"But—"

"All the other things—I think you're imagining them."

"What other things?"

"Your persecution complex."

"Only kidding."

"Quoting scripture."

"A lark."

"That look you get in your eyes."

"When?"

"Whenever the audience applauds."

"Is that so?"

She nodded. Was that a tear that appeared in her left eye? Perhaps there *was* something to what she said.

* * *

Hades was not just a place for evil men; it was a place for everyone. The Elysian Fields was in Hades, also known as Paradise, where heroic, kind, and noble people went when they died, a place of luxury and bliss. The Asphodel Fields were there, too. Relatively unheard of, this is where most people ended up. It was a dull, depressing place— shadowy, misty, and gray—where one led a dull, depressing existence as a soul who wandered forever through the shadows.

The main river flowing through Hades was the River Styx. Styx was a goddess, the daughter of Ocean. When Zeus summoned the gods to Olympus to help him fight the Titans, Styx was the first to come. She brought her children with her and as a reward Zeus ordained that she and her children should always live with him. Styx was the daughter of the mother of many monsters, Echidna, and her giant husband Typhon. Hades was the ruler of the underworld. He was the King of the Dead, a huge, menacing creature who had many adventures in his land. He abducted the maiden Persephone, tricked Theseus and Peirithous, and scuffled with Sisyphus before consigning him to his fate. Hades was so feared that he was given another less ominous-sounding name. That name was Pluto.

* * *

Perhaps. Definitely not. Perhaps.

Perhaps I *did* suffer from a persecution complex. Who wouldn't after being subjected to days and nights of adoration, followed by days and nights of abuse? (I am thinking of the pointless, never-ending questions to which I was subjected.)

No, I did not imagine I was God. I *could* have been God, I suppose, but I did not *imagine* I was Him. It was truer to say I was searching for God, that I had no idea where I would find Him—or even if I would find Him—but that I was willing to travel to the far reaches of the cosmos in my quest.

Perhaps I *was* crazy. If the truth be told, I'd considered the possibility. I'd also wondered if I was a genius. There is a thin line between insanity and genius and I had come to the conclusion that I no longer knew what side of that line I was on. And that I did not care.

* * *

When Orpheus went looking for his deceased bride, Eurydice, he sang so sweetly that Cerberus lay down and let him pass. Eurydice had been struck dead by a rattlesnake on her wedding day. And Orpheus set out to bring her back from the underworld, a feat few mortals ever achieved.

Orpheus' music was so divine that all the inhabitants of Hades stopped and listened to him sing. His words were enough to melt the heart of Persephone, the queen of the Underworld. She pleaded with her husband to let Orpheus bring Eurydice back to Greece.

If anyone should have known what Orpheus felt it was Persephone. She was a beautiful young woman, the daughter of Zeus and Demeter. Hades had heard many stories of her beauty from newcomers to his kingdom. His curiosity was aroused and eventually he could not resist the urge to see for himself. The moment he set eyes upon Persephone he knew she would have to become his bride. One day while she was collecting flowers on the plain of Enna, the earth opened and Hades rose up and abducted her. Demeter was broken-hearted when she learned what had happened. She was the goddess of the harvest and when she withdrew from the world in loneliness, the earth became infertile. Zeus ordered Hades to release Persephone. He agreed but bargained with his brother to have her live in the underworld for one-third of the year. When Persephone was in Hades, Demeter refused to let anything grow and winter commenced. The rest of the year Persephone lived with her mother.

* * *

I returned to Lowell a national hero and was offered a position as senior research scientist. I indicated my willingness to accept—but first wished to obtain an advanced degree. The University of Arizona had recently established a graduate program in Astronomy and Astrophysics and I was one of the first to matriculate, receiving my PhD in the spring of 1935.

Back to Lowell! Working nearly twenty-thousand hours over the next ten years, I studied planetary satellites and ring systems, comets, Kuiper Belt objects, the formation of stars, the interstellar medium, and evolutionary processes in the Milky Way and other galaxies. I published dozens of articles and received numerous awards.

It was in the summer of 1945 when I received the call. Harvard was offering me a two-year lectureship in the astronomy department. I was overjoyed. My duties would be simple. I would teach one class a semester and devote the rest of my time to research.

I had spent sixteen years in Flagstaff and it was difficult to leave, but this was an opportunity I could not turn down. The past years had been a time of reflection for both me and Isabella. The love between us only deepened. My epileptic fits seemed to have stabilized and now were little more than an annoyance.

I began my teaching career at Harvard in the fall of 1945. I enjoyed lecturing and my class was popular. Isabella loved Boston and with the university's help found employment as a secretary in the physics department.

It was later that semester when things started to go downhill. In hindsight I realize my epilepsy was rearing its ugly head once more, but at the time I had no idea what was happening. Occasionally during my lectures I would stare into space for minutes at a time. Once a student came up to me after class and asked if I was feeling all right. I assured her I was simply lost in thought, but the next day a member of the astronomy department asked me the same question. He mentioned something about paranoia. I remember laughing at his rather subtle attempt to question my sanity.

It was a gray day in December when I gave a talk to the faculty on the chemical composition of comets. I thought it a brilliant lecture. But the applause was not as enthusiastic as usual. I did not understand why and, to be honest, it frightened me. Looking back, I see what happened. This was not a lay audience to which I could end-lessly prattle, say anything that came into my head and be adored. No, these were learned men, men who had come to the conclusion that I was a fake.

I attended a party later in the evening. It was at the house of the chairman of the astronomy department. Red Butler. He was a jovial fellow, with red hair and sparkling blue eyes. A deep, baritone voice that boomed throughout the living room when he laughed. His wife was charming. I remember her asking how I'd liked Flagstaff. She hated Boston, she said. The winters were horrid and there were far too many people. I told her the winters in Arizona could be awful, too. And as for the people, well, it was all a matter of degree.

There was another fellow there to whom I took an in-stant dislike. While I was talking to Mrs. Butler, he took the opportunity to talk to my wife. I didn't like the looks of him. Slick, black hair. Immaculately dressed. A red carna-tion in his lapel. A true Jim Dandy. I couldn't hear what he was saying because he was on the other side of the room. But I knew what I thought he was saying.

* * *

Persephone looked at her husband and said, "You must make an exception and let Orpheus bring his love back with him. You must do this for me."

Hades could not deny his queen her request, and he agreed to let Orpheus bring Eurydice back on one condi-tion: that Orpheus should not look upon her until they were both back in the land of the living.

Doubt crept into Orpheus' mind as he made his as-cent. Plagued by thoughts that Hades had deceived him—was it not more likely that a wild beast was following?—Orpheus turned around to see Eurydice behind him. Without delay, the swift Hermes was there to lead her back to the underworld. Orpheus' heart broken, he returned to his homeland and lived in the forest for many years, making the wildlife cry with his sad music.

One day a band of wild Maenads, the followers of Dionysus, the god of wine, came upon Orpheus. Would he sing joyous songs so they could dance? When he refused, they worked themselves into a frenzy and tore him to pieces. They threw his body into a river that carried him out to sea—to the island of Lesbos. His mother, Calliope, lived there. When she saw it was her son's body that had washed ashore, she mourned him and gave him a proper burial.

* * *

Isabella is gone. Is it because I drank too much that night and had to be led away? Is it because I said something I shouldn't have said? They told me later that I was exhausted. That the rigors of academic life had proven too much. That I needed to rest. That was all. That was all, they said.

They put me in the hospital where I was watched by a three-headed dog. I slept for seven days and seven nights. I didn't want to see anyone. When the doctor woke me, he said I was cured. I could continue my research. I could discover the tenth planet. Or the eleventh. Or the twelfth. Or whatever else it was I felt I had to do.

I went back to Harvard to apologize and say my goodbyes. They said not to worry, that it happened to the best of men. A six-month sabbatical was what was called for, Dr. Butler said. A period of rest after which I could resume my research. What he meant to say, of course, was that I was washed up. That never again would I discover anything of importance. That no one cared about me anymore. I remember Mrs. Butler putting her arm around me and whispering into my ear, "Remember me."

It was all over, anyway. Harvard was the last stop. The end of the line. And when I went to find Isabella and was told that she had run off with someone else—an associate professor in the physics department—the cry of grief that escaped my lips could have been heard as far away as the ninth planet from the Sun. At that moment Pluto was the only place where I wanted to be.

$$* * *$$

Three days later I went to a psychologist. I couldn't eat. I couldn't think. My headaches were unbearable. I felt a weight pressing on my shoulders. I had to do something! And so, even though it was hard for me to admit I needed help, I sought help.

"My wife has left me," I told Dr. Turner, a thin, elderly man with a wispy white beard who looked at me compassionately from behind an oak desk. "And I don't know what to do."

"Do you know why she left?"

"That's just it—I don't."

I must not have sounded convincing for he added gently, "Are you sure?"

I looked at the floor. "I think Isabella believes I'm nuts."

"Why would she leave you if she thought that you were nuts?"

I hadn't thought of that. "I guess there must have been another reason," I said. "But I don't know what it is."

"And that's why you're here."

"Yes, that's why I'm here. I feel like I'm about to explode."

"You feel your life has been a failure?"

"I wouldn't go that far. I discovered Pluto, after all. And I discovered a black hole orbiting Earth. I'm not sure where it is now, though—it vanished unexpectedly—and that's a problem, because I would like to visit it one day."

"I see."

This was common knowledge; it shouldn't have surprised him.

He sighed and pulled out a pad and wrote something on it.

Then he said again, "I see."

I could see this was going nowhere.

"I feel like my life is in a thousand pieces," I continued. "I'm a mirror that's been shattered. I'm all jumbled up."

"Why might that be?"

"Maybe it's because I'm gone much of the time."

"The demands of your work, yes. I can only imagine the commitments of a man of your stature."

I wasn't about to tell him I was the laughingstock of the astronomy department and that I found solace in traveling to the farthest reaches of the cosmos. It would only have complicated matters. Instead I said, "Maybe my medical condition has something to do with it."

"Your medical condition?"

"I'm epileptic. I'm under a doctor's care and the disease is under control, or so the doctor tells me. No, that can't be the cause."

"You think, though, that it might be. Why do you think that?"

"The neural circuitry in my brain is a mess," I said. "It causes me to connect thoughts in strange ways. Where others go from A to B, I go from A to Q to J to V and maybe back to B. Or maybe not."

"Have you considered this might also be the cause of your creativity?"

"I'd never thought of it that way."

"It's not unusual for creative people to, shall we say, act bizarre."

"But in my case I fear it's indicative of something else."

"Why do you say that?"

"I blank out."

Dr. Turner looked concerned. "For long periods of time?"

"Days, perhaps weeks. I never really know."

"But surely . . ." He paused and scribbled something on his pad. "You mean, I presume, that for an extended period you feel lost."

I scratched my nose. Things were getting uncomfortable.

"Yes," I said. "That's one way to put it."

"Perhaps the result of an epileptic seizure?"

"I suppose."

"And what does your physician say?"

"That I must learn to live with them."

"Then that is that, I suppose. We must all learn to live with—"

"It's a bizarre experience to have a seizure," I interrupted. "You slip into another world. Your body is flapping around and you're biting your tongue and batting your head on the ground but your mind is somewhere else. What's most bizarre, though, is that it's impossible *not* to go there. To that other world. It's only when you realize you're comfortable in *this* place—this other place—that you're shocked back into reality." I jumped to my feet. "And that's where the trouble lies. I've learned to live with myself, but apparently Isabella has not. And that is what I don't understand. We were together for twenty years. She knew about my condition before we married. It meant nothing to her. She promised to stand by me when I was here—and when I wasn't."

Dr. Turner shifted uncomfortably in his chair. His velvety blue eyes looked at me earnestly. "Yes," he said. "Go on. I think we're getting somewhere."

I shrugged. "There's nothing else to say."

"Did you have any children?"

"No, we were childless," I lied. "I think Isabella resented it—that I was never there."

"You couldn't see yourself as a father, you mean?"

"Yes."

"I see. And—"

But I was through. "She left me, doctor. It's hopeless. I was a fool to think we could work things out." I paused, then added, "I'm not someone you can love."

"Surely you don't believe that."

Enough was enough. Without giving him a chance to continue, I rushed out the door, past an astonished secretary who had probably been listening to our every word.

"Would you like to schedule a second consultation?" she asked.

"That will not be necessary," I said. "I am cured. Dr. Turner is a brilliant man."

And with that I left the building, emerging onto a sunny Boston street. It was 4:30 in the afternoon and I had nowhere to go, nowhere to turn.

* * *

It is midnight. Orpheus gives the coin to Charon who ferries him across the River Styx. He sees Cerberus and passes through the gates of Hades. To his relief he is sent to the Elysian Fields. There he spies Eurydice in a meadow. It is as he hoped, as he had prayed for. He calls out to her. She turns and smiles. And there I shall leave them, gazing upon each other for eternity.

* * *

A week later Isabella returned. It was only a vacation, she said. A time for her to collect her thoughts. Did I know that she loved to write? Well, she wanted to make a go of it and had attended a writers retreat in New Hampshire. She hadn't told me because she thought I would disapprove. She blushed. It was nice to be home, though. Even so—she had to be honest—it had been good to get away for a while. I threw my arms around her and we kissed. Then I asked her about the other man. He was just an acquaintance, she laughed. No need to worry.

* * *

But I did worry. I couldn't stop worrying. So I swallowed my pride and returned to Dr. Turner.

"Isabella's back," I said. "She wants me to forgive her."

He smiled. "Why do you think that might be?"

I couldn't control myself. It was as if something snapped in my brain. My life's story came pouring out.

"I guess it begins at the beginning," I said. "Doesn't it always? Begin at the beginning . . .?"

He nodded.

"When I was a child," I continued, "I realized I was different. I thought differently. I felt differently. How do I explain it? I didn't think like other children. I thought about different things, like the immensity of the universe and what came before and how it would end. My time was preoccupied with trying to explain the unexplainable. What would happen if I fell into a black hole. Or traveled through interstellar space. Or burst through what lies at the end of the universe. Do you know what I'm saying?"

Another nod.

"These thoughts tormented me. I couldn't sleep at night. And when I tried to talk to others about them—why, I got nothing but strange looks in return. And that only made me feel more alone. I was fifteen, perhaps sixteen years old.

"It was when I went to college that things changed—and for the better. I met Isabella. She was the most intelligent person I had ever met. We went to the university observatory—I was an astronomy major and had a key to the building—I showed her the planets. Mars was prominent that evening. And Saturn. And Jupiter. I showed her the moons of Jupiter. She was awestruck. I told her I belonged there—among the planets and the stars. She laughed, but she wasn't making fun of me. I said—excitedly for I realized I was in the presence of a kindred spirit—that I belonged there, and that I went there too, sometimes for days at a time."

"What did she say?"

"The most amazing thing anyone had ever said to me. I shall never forget her words. 'There's nothing like gazing on the cradle of existence to put life in perspective.' And then she broke into a smile. A beautiful smile."

I felt waves of happiness sweeping over me as I recalled those days from long ago.

Eventually the doctor brought me out of my trance. "Perhaps you'd better tell me what happened next."

"We married."

"Were you happy?"

"I had never known such happiness."

"And then?"

"I found employment at Lowell and discovered the ninth planet of the solar system and became famous and traveled the country with Isabella and taught astronomy at Harvard and then everything fell apart."

"You sound bitter."

"Why do you say that?"

"The tone of your words."

"Wouldn't you be?"

He stroked his beard. His pale-blue eyes scanned me uneasily. "When were you diagnosed with epilepsy?"

"When I was twenty," I said. "Though I believe it began much earlier. The doctors didn't know what to do with me. I was an unusual case, they said. And they were right. You see, epilepsy causes a subtle alteration in brain waves. I found I was able to travel through the cosmos."

His eyes bulged. "You are speaking figuratively, of course."

"No."

He frowned. "You mean you are literally able to visit other worlds?"

"Yes."

"No wonder your wife left you!" Dr. Turner emitted a boisterous laugh.

I found his attempt at humor unsettling, but I managed to maintain my composure. "I would be lying if I said it didn't make things difficult," I continued. "I tried to get her to go with me every so often—to the moons of Jupiter, the Orion Nebula, the Andromeda Galaxy—but she never would. I don't know whether she thought my epilepsy had degraded my thought processes to the point where I could no longer think clearly or if she believed in my new powers and was simply too scared to accompany me—"

"Did you have seizures?"

"At that time?"

"Yes."

"I don't remember. I suppose it's possible."

Dr. Turner sighed. "I don't think I can do anything for you, Franz," he said. "I suggest you get advice from a neurologist."

"I have been, for many years."

"Has it occurred to you that you might need to see another doctor? I can give you several names. To be honest, Franz, I'm not convinced you're suffering from epilepsy. You're hallucinating. I have no idea what's causing your hallucinations. Perhaps it's due to epileptic seizures, perhaps something else. But you and I both know that space travel, such as you describe, is impossible. You can't simply will yourself to be elsewhere."

I glared. "So that's what you are getting at! You think that with my marriage crumbling and my career in jeopardy I'm unable to face reality. You think I'm running off to places that exist only in my mind. Has it occurred to you that I began suffering these hallucinations—as you call them—before any of those events occurred?"

He could not suppress a smile. "That, too, could be an illusion," he said.

"I wish I could go back in time, undo the past."

"But you can't."

"I wish I could."

"What would you change?"

* * *

Time travel is a subject I have not touched upon. I have always found it ironic that when I look up at the night sky I'm looking into the past. And when I travel to these past worlds the past becomes the present. In other words, I cannot travel backwards in time, only forwards. This to me is frustrating. It means I can look at the past, and imagine what transpired, but I can never go there. It tantalizes.

The space-time continuum is a joining of space and time. Think of it as the line one traces through space as time passes. This line (what I term a thread) is one of an infinite number of threads radiating from the point in space-time we call the present. Call this point A. I am free to pick which thread I wish at point A, but once I do so I cannot switch to another thread emanating from point A (this would involve traveling backwards in time). I arrive at point B and the process repeats.

Thus we have an infinite number of threads radiating from an infinite number of points, forming a cone that expands as time progresses. Whether these threads really exist or not is unknowable and irrelevant, for we can never know them nor they us.

However, let us assume they exist. This means there is not one universe, but many. There is a universe in which I am here. There is a universe in which I am there. There is a universe in which I am a famous astronomer. There is a universe in which I am a has-been. There is a universe in which Isabella and I live happily ever after. There is a universe in which we part.

* * *

I took the next semester off, as Dr. Butler had suggested, and returned in the fall of 1946. I felt rejuvenated and was eager to resume my teaching duties. I had a new research interest as well. The search for life on other worlds.

PSR B1620-26C

(September 17, 1946)

PSR B1620-26c is a planet orbiting the pulsar PSR B1620-26 in the constellation Scorpius. The pulsar is thirteen billion years old, nearly as old as the universe itself.

PSR B1620-26c is nearly three times as large as Jupiter, but, unlike Jupiter, it is a rocky world. It follows a circular orbit around the pulsar at a distance five times that of the earth from the Sun (about the distance of Uranus). It orbits the pulsar once every one hundred Earth years. I assumed it was a dead planet orbiting a dead sun. But perhaps it was not always that way.

When I pay PSR B1620-26c a visit, I discover there had been three other planets orbiting the sun-like star that became the pulsar. They are dead and gone now, vaporized when the pulsar formed. But when the universe was seven billion years old one of these planets—the one I dubbed Amore—supported life. From studying pictographs etched in huge cliffs, I learned that Amore had been a lush-green planet with countless hills and valleys and gently winding rivers. There were enormous plants of unknown variety, with strange orange blossoms which emitted exotic smells. Portions of the surface were covered with irregularly shaped gray boulders. The atmosphere was a mixture of carbon and oxygen. The sky was a work of art: hundreds of shimmering shades of pink and red. Of the inhabitants of Amore I uncovered little, only that they had been intelligent, could live on the land or in the sea, possessed a rudimentary language, and reproduced by means of spores. How sad that Amore had vanished, that its inhabitants were no longer there to greet me.

I spent days traveling across PSR B1620-26c. In a valley that opened onto an alluvial plain I came upon evidence of another civilization, perhaps descendants of the Amorean race. My heart leaped into my mouth. My journey had not been in vain! I saw buildings that looked like temples with spires and terraces and fountains. I saw dozens of smaller structures of various geometrical shapes: a perfect cylinder, a perfect sphere, a rhombus, a trapezoid, a seven-pointed star. The buildings were adorned with writings that resembled Egyptian hieroglyphics. Try as I might I could not decipher them.

I went into the seven-pointed star. The floor was covered with a fine ashy powder. I saw broken bottles and wooden objects that might once have been furniture. There was a doorway leading to another room and I started towards it, but then I heard a slithering noise, and I smelled something awful, a dank, putrid smell, like swamp water. I hurried outside into the light.

And I saw them. The inhabitants of PSR B1620-26c. Wriggling across the cracked pavement.

They looked like giant reptiles, hairless, with green skin, bulging skulls, enormous red eyes, three-fingered hands, six legs, and long tails covered with spikes. The species was thirty million years old (three billion Earth years), based on information I later extracted from the pictographs. I wondered how it could be possible that they had not advanced beyond the reptilian stage.

Then it struck me. How wrong had I been! These were not the first inhabitants of PSR B1620-26c. Another race had come before. A race which had built the temples and the other structures. A race which had come and gone.

VI

THERE IS NO LIFE ON MARS

They told me there was no life on Mars.

"How can that be!" I cried. "I discovered life on Mars. Primitive life, it's true, but life, nonetheless."

"No life. No life on Mars."

My experiments were flawless, my reasoning divine. How many days and nights did I toil? How many Martian soil samples did I sift through, looking for those infernal little Martians? And when I finally came upon them—so humanlike, so finely drawn—it was a true Eureka! moment and I knew what it would mean to mankind. But now— now!—you say I was mistaken?

"There is no life. No life on Mars."

No, it is *you* who are mistaken. I know what I discovered. Pygmy Joe and Pygmy Sue. They live near the polar ice caps. They are quite small—no taller than the width of my hand—I could easily have missed them; indeed, it was only on a second look that I spotted them. Joe is a thin fellow with wavy, light-brown hair and a long beard. He dresses smartly in a freshly-pressed shirt and trousers, black shoes. He is always the gentleman as he sweeps his top hat before him to salute Sue. She dresses simply in a white blouse and plain skirt. There is a shawl around her shoulders and she wears a blue bonnet. They seem not to notice me when I bend down to greet them.

"There is no life. No life on Mars."

The pygmy's language is a confusing mix of grunts and monosyllabic sounds like *ta* and *da* and *rhu*. And it is only after many visits that I am able to decipher their language. Here is a sample of conversation:

Joe, you look well today.
Thank you, Sue. And isn't the weather fine?
Oh, yes. Fine, oh so fine!
How are your parents?
I have not seen them for some time. They live far away.
How sad.
Yes.
Sue?
Yes.
Would you be my wife?
Why, Joe! I didn't know you felt that way about me.
But I do . . . I do feel that way. And I want to be with you . . . always.
I'm flattered.
So will you? Will you be mine?
Why, I think I just might!

And now I, Franz Herbert, discoverer of the ninth planet from the Sun, will leave my pygmies where I found them. They will marry, I am sure, and have little pygmies. For there *is* life. There is life on Mars.

* * *

"Isabella," I asked. "Do you think I'm crazy?"
"Of course not," my wife said as she patted my hand.
I sighed. "Do you know what it's like to be ridiculed?"

Her brown eyes looked at me uncomprehendingly.

"No," I said. "I guess you don't." I paused. "Well, let me tell you. Let me tell you what it's like to be ridiculed. Imagine that I'm a fish. A fish traveling up a river, perhaps to spawn. Fisherman and men with spears line the shores. They aim their spears at me and laugh as they try to kill me. 'Look at the little fish as it twists and turns,' they cry, 'flaying wildly, trying to avoid death. It really is a plump little fish; we could cook it for our dinner!'"

Isabella rolled her eyes. "Franz—be serious."

"Yes, I discovered Pluto. And I was applauded for my discovery. Famous—for a time—though I never sought fame. But—let's be honest—anyone could have discovered that planet. Anyone with enough time and perseverance. But life on Mars—Mars!—now *that* was a real discovery. A discovery that was mine and mine alone."

"Franz," she interjected. "Let's take a trip."

A trip!

"Well," I said after a moment's reflection. "I hear the Andromeda Galaxy is nice this time of year. But if that's too far, Saturn has a dozen moons that would do. For a weekend getaway."

"Hmm."

"Have I ever told you about Hyperion?"

"No."

"Hyperion is a beautiful place, endless clouds of gas and dust, a birthplace of stars and civilizations. It is far away—beyond the quasars that exist at the outer reaches of the universe, beyond the blackness that lies beyond space. Would you consider—"

"Not now, Franz. Perhaps another time."

* * *

In 1877, the Italian astronomer Giovanni Schiaparelli mapped the Martian surface. His illustrations showed a system of features which he called *canali*, meaning channels. The word was translated into English as canals—implying an artificial feature, though this was not what Schiaparelli intended.

The idea fascinated Percival Lowell, who had recently graduated from Harvard University with a degree in mathematics. The man was a true polymath. He published a groundbreaking article on the nebular hypothesis, traveled to Europe and the Middle East, then returned to Boston to run the family cotton mill. Six years later he became a foreign secretary and moved to the Far East, spending time in South Korea and Japan. He came back to the United States in 1893 and founded Lowell Observatory in Flagstaff, Arizona. For the next fifteen years he studied Mars extensively, refining Schiaparelli's maps and putting forth the theory that the canals were the result of Martian activity. He published three books on the subject: *Mars* (1895), *Mars and its Canals* (1906), and *Mars as the Abode of Life* (1908).

His ideas were accepted for a time and even inspired H. G. Wells to write *The War of the Worlds*, a fantastic novel about an invasion by Martians desperate for water to fill the canals on their arid and dying planet.

But subsequent observations showed that the canals were simply optical illusions and it didn't help when Giovanni himself called Percival an idiot.

* * *

Isabella and I found ourselves the subject of ridicule. "Don't worry," I said in an attempt to alleviate her concerns. "The ideas of great men are often scorned."

She said, "I know." But she *looked* worried.

"Perhaps it is the epilepsy," I said. "Perhaps my brain is turning to mush."

"Franz, please! Don't be silly."

"I'm serious. The doctor said that in the advanced stage of this disease, the brain turns to mush."

"You're thinking of rabies."

"No, I'm certain he was speaking of epilepsy. It's strange, Isabella. I've lived with this disease for so long I've learned to accept it. Live with it. Control it. But lately I've been wondering . . . perhaps it's really controlling me?"

"As in consuming you? Turning your brain to mush?"

I nodded. "I may be going mad."

* * *

Pluto was named by Venetia Burney, an eleven-year-old girl from Oxford, England. She was interested in Greek and Roman mythology and thought that Hades, the Greek god of the underworld, was an appropriate name since the mysterious planet lived so far out in the solar system. A planetary underworld. The name Pluto was used to match the Roman names of the other planets.

The abbreviation for Pluto is "PL," the first two letters of the planet's name, though it's also Percival Lowell's initials (a remarkable coincidence, wouldn't you say?). Percival tried in vain to discover the planet in the early years of the twentieth century. Indeed, he devoted the last eight years of his life to the search. At Lowell Observatory in Flagstaff, Arizona.

It was Percival's own hypothesis. He predicted a planet beyond Neptune based on discrepancies between the predicted and observed positions of Neptune and Uranus, and the erroneous assumption that such discrepancies were caused by the gravitational influence of an unknown planet. In point of fact, the discrepancies were due to erroneous values for the masses of Neptune and Uranus. From the beginning it was a futile search.

But it did not deter Percival. He plodded ahead year after year, getting nowhere, but refusing to question his hypothesis. In time, even his colleagues began to have doubts. They talked behind his back. One of the chief scientists laughed openly and said that Percival's best days were behind him. Percival took the criticism to heart and from then on devoted his days to administrative tasks. But one weekend evening someone found him at the telescope, scanning the heavens in search of his undiscovered planet. He looked chagrined, and insisted he was only scanning the sky for comets. No one believed him. And that was the end of Percival's quest; though upon his deathbed in 1916 he maintained that a ninth planet existed.

You see, life admits only one great discovery. For Percival, his was the discovery of life on Mars. The irony was that though his discovery was ridiculed at the time, it turned out to be true. He second quest—the search for Pluto—failed.

Percival Lowell did not discover Pluto. I did. And what I discovered was a peanut-sized planet, one too small to exert any appreciable gravitational force on other planets. What did this imply about Pluto? That it was a planetary afterthought? Insignificant and without consequence? Undoubtedly. For if Pluto didn't exist, nothing about the solar system would change. And that meant my discovery of the planet was without consequence as well.

* * *

"There is no life. No life on Mars."

Mars' polar ice caps are composed of frozen carbon dioxide. But they thaw in the summer months. And that is when life emerges onto the surface. It had been there all along, deep in the volcanoes that dot the Martian surface at the lower latitudes. There the temperatures are conducive to life. There the pygmies live. They have constructed elaborate labyrinths which lead from the volcanoes to the polar caps. And it is there that the pygmies obtain water in the summertime when the polar caps melt. They carry the water back to the volcanoes and fill huge vats for the remainder of the year.

I have visited these volcanoes. I have descended deep inside. I have seen the giant cisterns and the labyrinths and the temples of the pygmies where they worship. Quite remarkable feats of engineering for creatures that are no more than six inches tall!

$$* * *$$

My arrival home was unexpected. I had suffered a ferocious headache in class, and at the conclusion of my lecture, I told the secretary I would be leaving early. I was in such pain I forgot to call Isabella and tell her I would be coming home. As I normally would have done.

When I got home, I saw them. Isabella and the refrigerator repairman. They were in the kitchen and he was writing up a bill. They were chatting about something banal like the weather, but right away I knew something was wrong. Perhaps it was the flirtatious tone of her voice. Or the look of complicity in his eyes.

I said nothing. I stood in the doorway and watched.

When the repairman was finished he handed Isabella the bill. "Give us a call if it acts up again," he said.

She smiled. "I'm sure it will be fine."

She was not holding his arm—it was true—but his arm was there, waiting to be held.

"What's wrong?" I asked, announcing my presence.

She looked up, startled.

"Franz?"

I repeated the question.

"It gave out this morning."

"Good-day to you both." The repairman latched his toolbox, tipped his hat, and was gone.

"He said the condenser coil was shot," Isabella explained. "We're lucky they could fit us in."

I retreated to the living room. I didn't want to hear another word.

* * *

"You—Franz Herbert—are a fool. You say you discovered Pluto, though that was not your work. It was Percival Lowell's. He provided you with the data. He told you where to look and what to look for. You were simply a tool. Anyone could have done what you did. Hardly the work of a great man. An original thinker. And your insistence of life on Mars? An absurdity. There is no life. No life on Mars!"

* * *

I thought of returning to Dr. Turner but decided against it. Instead, I called my personal physician, the man who had treated my epilepsy for many years, Dr. Strike.

"Franz," he said as he clapped me on the shoulder. "How are you getting along these days?"

"Not good," I replied. "I've been to a psychologist and he thinks I'm nuts."

Dr. Strike has a booming laugh; it echoes off walls and cascades down hallways. He slapped his thigh and exclaimed, "Why, I've been telling you that for years."

I smiled. "Dr. Turner thinks I'm delusional, that I don't really have epilepsy."

"I can emphatically tell you that is wrong," Dr. Strike said. "Tests have confirmed your condition. You know this, Franz."

"My wife has been unfaithful to me," I said. "Is that why I can't think straight?"

"I'm sorry," he said. "It happens to the best of men. It makes your illness harder to handle, of course. But it doesn't change the fact that you suffer from a mild form of the disease."

I should tell you right off that I had never told Dr. Strike about my cosmic travels. I had known him for three decades and had never breathed a word of them to him. In fact, the only person I had ever told—besides Isabella—was Dr. Turner. And you saw where that got me.

"I confronted Isabella last night," I said. "We argued. She packed her bags and left. She's running off with the refrigerator repairman."

Dr. Strike shrugged. "My advice to you is to quit worrying. Your medication is working. Wives leave husbands. Husbands leave wives. Discoveries are made and forgotten. It's all part of the fabric of life." He laughed. "I'm out of my league here, of course, but I'd say you're doing pretty fine, Franz!"

"I don't feel that way."

"Your problem is that you think too much. If you didn't think about the cosmos, you wouldn't feel lost in space. I'm speaking to you as a friend, not a doctor, as I have no formal training in psychology. But consider this: all of us are lost in space, adrift in a universe that seems cold and cruel." He paused, then added, "Have you considered seeing a second psychologist? There are several I can recommend."

I looked at him coldly.

"Other than that, Franz," he concluded, "there is nothing you can do but take your medicine!"

My psychologist tells me to see a physician. My physician tells me to see a psychologist. It's no wonder I escape to the cosmos. It's the only place where I can be alone.

* * *

I met the pygmies and held council with their leader. He is an interesting man, taller than the rest, perhaps a full foot in height. He wears a turban and a cloak of animal origin. He has pale-blue eyes, thick lips, and coarse black hair. He calls the tribe (this is how they refer to themselves) together twice a week. Incense burns in the cavern where they gather. It is a dark place, deep in the heart of a dead volcano. The members of the tribe call out to him and there is weeping and ululating. His voice is deep and powerful. He speaks for thirty minutes. No one interrupts him. I have no idea what he says, for he talks in a dialect I do not understand. When he is done, the tribe files out. I never heard a single person question his words.

When the last pygmy left, I approached the leader and bowed before him. He looked up at me in awe (remember: I was nearly six feet taller) but said nothing.

"I am a stranger," I said. "Tell me what has taken place here."

To my surprise he replied in perfect English: "I am the leader of the tribe of the Wakaw. We are the last descendants of the original Martian race."

I raised my eyebrows.

"Once this planet was teaming with life," he continued. "In the time of the giants. But the giants died—a dreaded disease they could not control. It made their women infertile. It choked the life from their race. Only the pygmies survived, but we shall fare no better. I am the last leader, the King of the Wakaw. When I pass, there will be no more."

And it was then I realized that I had never seen a child on Mars.

He continued with words that alarmed me:

"Percival Lowell was right. The canals he saw were real. They carried water to our cities, as he maintained. But too late we realized they also transported the agents of our death: deadly microbes from the outer reaches of the galaxy that have destroyed us."

He looked tired. I left him then and returned to the planet's surface. It looked like a wasteland. The winds were howling and the sky was thick with red dust. I climbed into my spaceship and blasted off. I would never come back to Mars.

* * *

It's no fun living in an empty apartment, but at least I have my beloved feline for company. Everywhere I look I see things that remind me of Isabella!

I lie on the couch with Pluto snuggled beside me. I hear his gentle purr. I can hardly believe it, but he is eighteen years old. An aging tomcat.

"Oh, Pluto," I lament. "Whatever shall we do?"

His purr is regular. For some reason, I am reminded of the ticking of a clock. As I pet him, his purring grows louder. And I notice something else: the purring seems to oscillate, growing louder then softer, louder then softer, and that the frequency between purrs remains constant. I wonder if that is true of all felines. A universal principle.

I am wondering how I can apply this to the universe at large when I recall Albert Einstein and his theory of general relativity. Of quantum theory. And the universal conundrum they pose.

General relativity describes the physics of the universe. Quantum theory describes the very small. And it is at the level of the very small that the theories come into conflict. It has to do with black holes.

General relativity says that at the center of a black hole lies a singularity, a point of infinite density where time stops. Quantum theory says it is no such thing: the center of a black hole is a smear of mathematical probabilities. Where time starts.

And I wonder: what is the true nature of time?

* * *

My therapists at the rehabilitation center told me: diaries are often good things to undertake. To determine the where, the when, the why, and the how. They urged me to take up my pen and record the day's events. What they don't know is that I've always done this; my life has been a series of diary entries.

* * *

I didn't tell Dr. Turner about Jason because I didn't want him to know what had happened to my son. If I'd told him, he would only have asked further questions, like: "Where is he now?" and "What is he doing?" In truth, I don't know. Jason ran off to the underworld when he turned seventeen. Intending to marry Eurydice. There was nothing I could have done to stop him.

If I'd revealed that, and lamented the heartbreak it caused, Dr. Turner would have dismissed me with a sigh. Just as Isabella dismissed me. With a wave of her hand.

Before I left Earth for the final time there was one thing I had to do. I promised Dr. Strike I would take a night off from my astronomical studies and go out on the town. I would do something different, something that might take my mind off my troubles. I went to the movies. *Gone With the Wind* was playing at the downtown cinema. I remember trudging through a thick blanket of snow that had fallen the day before, snow that sparkled in the bright yellow light cast from streetlamps.

The theater was packed and it took nearly a minute before I found an empty seat near the back. I must have gotten the starting time wrong for the show seemed to be well along. I settled back into my seat and drank up the images that flowed before me:

Scarlett: Rhett! Rhett, where are you going?

Rhett: I'm going back to Charleston, back where I belong.

Scarlett: Please, please take me with you!

Rhett: No, I'm through with everything here. I want peace. I want to see if somewhere there isn't something left in life of charm and grace. Do you know what I'm talking about?

Scarlett: No! I only know that I love you.

Rhett: That's your misfortune.

[Rhett turns to walk down the stairs]

Scarlett: Oh, Rhett!

[Scarlett watches Rhett walk to the door]

Scarlett: Rhett!

[She runs down the stairs after Rhett]

Scarlett: Rhett, Rhett!

[catches him as he's walking out the front door]

Scarlett: Rhett . . . if you go, where shall I go, what shall I do?

Rhett: Frankly, my dear, I don't give a damn.

[He walks off into the fog]

Their words hung in midair, shimmering in silence. I looked around me, couples everywhere, smiling and holding hands. I realized the time had come. I rose and left the theater. And then I was gone.

THREE DEGREES ABOVE ABSOLUTE ZERO

(January 3, 1947)

As old as they are, quasars were not the first stellar objects to have formed in the universe. We know light travels at a finite speed, 186,000 miles per second. Distant objects appear to our eyes not as they are but as they once were: the Sun as it was eight minutes ago, nearby stars as they were several years ago, the Andromeda Galaxy as it was two million years ago, quasars as they were twelve billion years ago.

Even so, quasars are not the most distant objects. Cosmic microwave background photons were emitted 400,000 years after the Big Bang, a billion years earlier than the photons from quasars. They are responsible for ionizing the gas which filled the early universe.

The early universe was a very hot place. As it expand-ed—two hundred years after the Big Bang—the gas within it began to cool. This radiation is literally the heat that is left over from the Big Bang. No longer hot, it is now about three degrees above absolute zero. It cannot be seen with the naked eye and is evident today as cosmic microwave background radiation. And it is everywhere. Think about that. The remains of the Big Bang are within arm's reach.

It gets weirder. Density equals mass cubed. When the universe was half its present size, the density of matter was eight times greater. The cosmic background radiation was twice as hot. When the universe was one hundredth its present size, the density of matter was one million times greater and the cosmic microwave background radiation was a hundred times hotter—approximately three hundred degrees above absolute zero—the temperature at which water freezes. Can you imagine what that was like? When the universe was one hundred millionth its present size, its temperature was scalding—273 million degrees above abso-lute zero; the density of matter was comparable to the den-sity of air at the earth's surface. We are near the beginning of time.

Ah, but we can never see that far back! Let me see if I can explain: In the beginning light and matter were not dis-tinct entities. They were indistinguishable from one another, having formed a dense, opaque plasma composed of free electrons, nuclei, and photons. It was like a wall steadily moving outwards. The behavior of this light/matter mov-ing through the early universe is analogous to the propaga-tion of light through the earth's atmosphere. Think of the plasma as a cloud surrounding the universe. On a cloudy day on Earth we can look through the air at the clouds, but we can not see through them. In the same way we can look back through the universe to a time when it was opaque:

400,000 years after the Big Bang. But we can see no further. It is a wall beyond which we cannot go.

One day I intend to go up to that wall. And then I will pass right through (remember: it is a wall only in the sense that a cloud is a wall). I know this will mean the end of me —that I will never return. But I don't care. For beyond that wall are sights no man has ever seen.

VII

THE DISTANCE TO THE GALAXIES

In the spring of 1947, I was given a lab. And a project: to determine the distance to the galaxies. The university had come into possession of a thromboscope, a device that could be used in conjunction with Cepheid variables to determine the distances to the galaxies. The theory had been all worked out, they said; what remained was to apply the theoretical constructs, and, with the aid of the thromboscope, to compile a comprehensive catalogue of stellar distances. The work would be tedious and would require the ability to detect minute changes in celestial motion. Since that was the method I had used to discover Pluto, they felt this was the perfect assignment.

I readily agreed to their request. It was a topic which interested me—galactic distance—and anyway, it would take my mind off Isabella, who had disappeared into the mists of time and space.

I would have no teaching duties that semester, and although it was never overtly stated, I knew why. Those disturbing incidents which had occurred fall semester. I "seized up" in social interactions: in my classes, at the departmental picnic party, at a downtown bar. I seemed to vanish from the stage. It involved my brain, the doctors told Isabella the day I was released from the hospital. It was unstable.

My wife informed Professor Butler. He said the department would do the prudent thing: They would isolate me. Exile me. Pretend as if I didn't exist. Because I didn't. Exist.

"Your student evaluations came in today," Professor Butler said the day before winter break began. I was seated in a green armchair in his office. He was pacing the floor. A frown on his wrinkled face.

"I don't know what to say," I stammered. "It was only an introductory class . . . I have no formal training in education . . . and then there's my unease . . ."

He nodded. "Perhaps . . ."

That was one of the last things Isabella spoke of, when we were having our final ferocious fight. My inability to relate to people. My preference to be *out there*, in the universe, rather than *in here*, where reality lies. "But isn't *in here* part of the universe as well?" I said. "And my traveling *out there* merely an extension?"

"You know what I mean, Franz!" she cried. And I guess I did know. And perhaps she was right. I've always felt more comfortable when I'm alone. . . .

And now I was back at Harvard with a project tossed to me like a bone to a dog. What was I to tell my colleagues? I had no use for their thromboscope or their well-formulated theories. I *knew* the distances to the galaxies. I *went* to them in my spaceship. Why, my odometer was accurate to a tenth of a light-year!

I could have told them all this, of course, but it would only have invited ridicule. And so I said nothing. I took up the thromboscope, trained my telescope on a far-flung galaxy, and began.

* * *

My first voyage was to ESO 269-57, a spiral galaxy in the constellation Centaurus, estimated to be one hundred light-years from Earth. It was a spectacular object, over 200,000 light-years across, consisting of two tightly wound inner spirals surrounded by a pair of outer arms that resembled mirror-reflections of each other. It was, to say the least, mesmerizing.

Nearly three-quarters of all galaxies are spirals. The Andromeda Galaxy is a spiral, the Pinwheel Galaxy is a spiral, the Sombrero Galaxy is a spiral. So is our own Milky Way.

Spiral arms are blue and blue-white because they contain hot young stars; they are regions of active star formation. The nucleus of spiral galaxies is red because it contains older stars. But it is the spiral arms which predominate, and it is the gravitational attraction between the stars within them which cause the arms to keep their spiral pattern.

Spirals come in many types. There are spiral galaxies with tightly wound arms and spiral galaxies with loosely wound arms. There are spirals with round centers and spirals with centers that look like bars. There is one characteristic they share, however: they all look like spinning pinwheels in the heavens.

Distance to ESO 269-57: My odometer showed that the galaxy was actually 250 light-years away.

The next five galaxies I visited were spirals as well. But the seventh was an elliptical. A glorious elliptical!

* * *

Desperate times call for desperate measures. First there was the refrigerator repairman, then the associate physics professor. How many others might there have been? Perhaps none, perhaps dozens. I had to know!

Then again—I could entertain the thought—perhaps Isabella had *not* been complicit, but, rather, had been seduced. If so, was I to blame? For being away so often. And for so long. No wonder my wife had succumbed. . . .

"Yes?"

The Watlin Detective Agency was in downtown Boston. A shabby second floor office in an old building on Province Street. The portly man I found myself facing motioned me to a leather-backed chair. "Mr. . . .?"

"Herbert. Franz Herbert. You are Mr. Watlin, I presume?"

He nodded.

Watlin glanced at a sheet of paper on his desk. "It says here that you wish us to investigate your wife." He eyed me closely. Studying me. Probing my mind. "What's troubling you?"

I told him the entire story. I was an astronomer professor, I said, but had fallen on hard times. There had been a medical emergency. A nervous breakdown. As for Isabella . . . I was certain of nothing, but I feared the worst. "It was as if we were navigating treacherous waters," I stammered. "It wasn't going well."

"I'm not sure I understand."

"Our marriage was on the rocks."

"I see." Watlin wrote something on the sheet of paper. "When did you last see Mrs. Herbert?"

"Last December. She said she was going to the grocery store. She never returned. Several days later I learned she had moved in with a visiting professor in the physics department. As I said, our marriage wasn't going well, but I never thought . . ."

"Have you attempted to contact her?"

"No."

"Is there anything else you wish to tell me?"

"The professor left Harvard at the end of the semester. I assume she went with him." I looked away. "I'll never forget the looks they exchanged at the departmental Christmas party. I tried not to believe . . ."

"You said he was a visiting professor. From where?"

"The Max Plank Institute of Astronomy in Heidelberg, Germany. Perhaps he returned there."

"That's where we'll start." Watlin smiled. "We'll be in touch, Mr. Herbert. I don't think this will take long."

* * *

IC 1101 is one of the largest known elliptical galaxies, one billion light-years distant. It was discovered in 1790 by Frederick Hershel and is the oldest known elliptical. There is a supermassive black hole at the center, a black hole I hope to visit one day. . . .

Elliptical galaxies are old and red, and with little gas or dust, there is virtually no star formation. They may have been spirals once, but, if so, the spiral arms collapsed into the central core. Many ellipticals are the result of collisions of two other galaxies.

They come in many shapes: circular, oblong, long, or narrow, and range in size from ten light-years to over a million in diameter.

Distance to IC 1101: My odometer showed that the estimated distance to the galaxy was essentially correct: 1.04 billion light-years.

After IC 1101 I went to several other ellipticals. They were all the same: cold, dead (or dying) places. Haunted by the end of things.

✳ ✳ ✳

My preliminary results were met with stony silence. The thromboscope was a difficult device to manage, I told a group of faculty members one March afternoon in the astrophysics conference room. And Cepheid variables were notoriously unreliable as celestial distance markers. Instead of tackling that problem, I came up with another method, one that could be used in conjunction with the thromboscope, but without the inconsistencies of Cepheids.

"What inconsistencies?" The question, by Professor Sid, an expert on star formation, was like a shot across the bow.

I tried to explain.

Cepheid variables were discovered in 1912 by the American astronomer Henrietta Leavitt. Through painstaking research, she determined that pulsations in the luminosity of the stars could be used to determine distance. It worked this way: Cepheids were variable stars that changed brightness according to a regular pattern, known as the star's period. They literally grew and shrunk in size, changing in brightness—or magnitude—as they did so.

The thromboscope was used to precisely measure a Cepheid's period. This was compared with other known Cepheids to determine its absolute magnitude (how bright it would appear at a standard distance). Next, the apparent magnitude was determined (how bright it looked to an observer on Earth—to Franz Herbert). The distance could be determined using the following equation:

$$m - M = 5 \log d - 5$$

Known as the distance modulus equation, where m is the apparent magnitude, M the absolute magnitude, and d the distance in parsecs.

118

There was, of course, a catch. The method assumed all Cepheids behaved identically, and I knew from my travels that that was not the case. There was no chart of standard Cepheid behavior, or, more specifically, there was a chart but it was wrong.

Arthur Eddington, in 1917, proposed that a heat-engine was the cause of Cepheid pulsations. He named the engine an Eddington-valve. In normal stars, temperature and pressure are balanced, an increase in one causing a decrease in the other, but in Cepheids an increase in temperature causes the pressure to increase as well, causing the star to expand until the excess energy dissipates, at which point the star contracts. It is like the valve in a locomotive only on a stellar scale. Eddington maintained that all valves behaved identically and were thus predictive in nature.

"But there's a problem," I said. "And it has to do with the nature of light. While light has constant velocity, it does not have constant luminosity. It's the variability of Cepheids which renders them useless, for there's no way of determining the luminosity of a light beam at any point in time."

Professor Sid scoffed. "You wish to disregard thirty-five years of established science! And your solution is to . . .?"

"Go there."

There was a collective gasp from the assembled.

"You are speaking figuratively, of course."

"Well, that would be the ideal solution."

"Mr. Herbert!"

I gazed at the distinguished members of Harvard's astrophysics department. Two dozen concerned, and perhaps troubled, faces. I felt pulled between the here and the there, and I struggled to stay firmly rooted to the earth.

"Yes," I said when the feeling passed. "The thromboscope is the key. One can compensate for the variability of light—and of the star—with a sufficient number of properly timed measurements. That's what I'm concentrating on now. I feel certain that, in the near future, my work will deliver—"

I felt the cold hand of Professor Butler upon me, ushering me back to my seat in the front row. There was polite applause and the chairman said something about looking forward to my final results. Results in which he had the utmost confidence.

The sarcasm could not have been more damning.

* * *

Lenticular galaxies look like spirals with the arms cut off, that is, they have a central bulge, but no spiral arms. They can be difficult to distinguish from elliptical galaxies—until you get up close.

Like elliptical galaxies, they consist of mainly older stars. They contain more gas and dust then ellipticals, however, and therefore can be seen as intermediaries between spirals and ellipticals.

The Cartwheel Galaxy is an excellent example. It was the place I visited next, 500 million light-years away in the constellation Sculptor. When I reached the galaxy I had a surprise. It turns out the Cartwheel was a spiral galaxy once but had been transformed *into* a lenticular!

And there was more.

A ring! A ring galaxy! There is a beautiful bluish ring that surrounds the Cartwheel, the result of a collision with a smaller galaxy 200 million years before. The collision stripped the Cartwheel of its spiral arms, chopping them off as it were, and changing its shape. The smaller galaxy is gone (I may try to track it down one day), but the Cartwheel remains, spinning slowly in the heavens like its namesake.

Distance to the Cartwheel Galaxy: My odometer read 502 million light-years.

$$* * *$$

"You found her?"

"We have."

"In Germany?"

"No."

I shot Watlin a look of surprise.

"She turned up in Stockholm."

I hesitated. "Was she alone?"

"She was."

It wasn't the answer I expected and I felt relieved. Unfortunately, the feeling wouldn't last.

"Our man spotted your wife in The English Bookshop in downtown Stockholm."

"Sweden! How did she—"

"What led us to her is no concern of yours. We have our methods."

I uttered a sigh of resignation.

"She was perusing the magazine section. Our man observed her for a quarter of an hour. Then she left the store. As I said, she was unaccompanied."

"Perhaps she was traveling through the country on her way to the states." I said. "Perhaps she meant to return to Boston. Perhaps a reunion is in order . . ." I was grasping at straws and I'm sure Watlin knew it.

"Further investigation revealed she was living with a Dr. Hans Bildt. A Swedish diplomat."

I felt knots forming in my stomach. "Of course," I said.

Watlin forced a smile. "I'm sorry. I know that's not the news you hoped to hear."

I rose and was turning to go, when Watlin added:

"If you'd be so kind as to make your check payable to Watlin Detective Agency, and hand it to Miss Cummings on your way out . . ."

I didn't want to hear any more. Without acknowledging his request, I was gone.

* * *

Three percent of the galaxies in the universe are not spirals, ellipticals, or lenticulars. They have irregular shapes and are termed Irregular Galaxies. They can be the result of collisions or near misses with other galaxies which, as you can imagine, scramble them in unusual ways.

The Small Magellanic Cloud is one of the more well-known irregulars. It lies in the constellation Tucana and is 200,000 light-years from the Milky Way. It looks like a cloud in the heavens. And that is what it was thought to be when it was discovered, during Magellan's first voyage around the world in 1520. Its precise distance was calculated in the eighteenth century; my odometer showed that the distance was more or less correct. As I zoomed by, I noted that there was a bridge of light connecting the Small Magellanic Cloud with its companion, the Large Magellanic Cloud. An interstellar highway, conveying material from one galaxy to the other. It really is amazing: the more I see of the universe, the more it resembles a gigantic multicellular organism!

The irregular dwarf galaxy PGC 16389 is another fine example, and it was my next stop. It looked like a small blob in the sky as I zeroed in on it. It must have been transformed by the collision with a second galaxy, for I saw another close by. I saw the guts of PGC 16389—pieces of its lost spiral arms—hanging off the center of the second galaxy.

Distance to PGC 16389: here the estimates were wildly off. It was not 150 million light-years, as the astronomers had pegged it; it was, in fact, 750 million light-years away.

* * *

I was in my office at Harvard, re-reading Eddington's tome *The Internal Constitution of the Stars* when the news was delivered: my appointment at Harvard had not been renewed. I could rest easy, however, Professor Butler told me. There was another position. At another place. It had all been arranged.

And what of my project, the distance to the galaxies? Work was proceeding at a steady clip and I felt certain the paper I was preparing would be well-received. I hinted at discoveries of an explosive nature. Discoveries that were certain to bring renown to the department.

There was no reply. The chairman had left.

Later that evening, in my apartment on Forty-Second Street, my beloved Pluto stretched out in my lap, I realized the answer to a question that had been plaguing me for years: the relationship between time and space was asymptotic, that is, the distance between two galaxies was non-linear. Like beams of light reflected in the mirrors of a carnival funhouse, distance was ephemeral and nearly impossible to pin down. And that was why light beams seemed to be everywhere at once. Because they were.

The mathematics necessary to work out the relationship between beams of light as they crisscrossed the cosmos would be difficult and I was not sure I was up to the task. But I was determined to try.

* * *

Isabella has left—but *has* she left? Or is it I who have fled, departing on a beam of light into the distant cosmos?

NEPTUNE

(February 11, 1948)

Neptune is the outermost gas giant. It has an equatorial diameter of 30,760 miles. If Neptune were hollow, it could contain nearly sixty Earths. Neptune orbits the Sun every 165 years. It has eight moons. Neptune, like Jupiter and Saturn but unlike Uranus, has an internal heat source. It produces 2.7 times more heat than it absorbs. It was discovered on September 23, 1846 by Johann Galle and Louis d'Arrest, an astronomy student, through mathematical predictions made by Urbain Jean Joseph Le Verrier.

The innermost two-thirds of Neptune is composed of a mixture of molten rock, water, liquid ammonia, and methane. The outer third is a mixture of hydrogen, helium, water, and methane. Methane gives Neptune its blue cloud color.

Neptune is a dynamic planet with large, dark spots reminiscent of Jupiter's hurricane-like storms. The largest spot, known as the Great Dark Spot, is about the size of Earth. It is a small, irregularly shaped, eastward-moving cloud scooting around the planet every sixteen hours or so. (That is the length of a Neptunian day.) This "scooter," as I have dubbed it, is a plume of cirrus clouds rising above a deeper cloud deck.

The strongest winds on any planet in the solar system occur on Neptune. Most of the winds blow westward, opposite the rotation of the planet. Near the Great Dark Spot winds blow up to 1,200 miles an hour.

Neptune has a set of four rings which are narrow and very faint. The rings are made up of dust particles thought to have been made by tiny meteorites smashing into Neptune's moons. They are dark and eerily beautiful.

Those are the facts, anyway, as reported in the scientific journals. And there is much more. But I am here to tell you something else. Something no one knows but me. There is an old man on the planet. I have spoken to him. He is called Neptune and he carries a trident.

Neptune lives on an island named Ajax. He is the only inhabitant. There is a temple on the island called Circus Flaminius. This is where I came upon him. He was gazing out at the deep-blue ocean. The ocean which is the planet Neptune.

He saw me approach but did not seem alarmed. And why should he have been? I looked like a harmless, gentle fellow.

I called out, "Hello there!"

He smiled.

I told him I was from the planet Earth and was studying the cosmos.

"I am searching for something," I said.

"And what might that be?"

"For a secret to tell Isabella."

"Isabella?"

"My wife."

"You are wasting your time."

I shook my head. "No," I said. "The universe is full of secrets. Why, I've just come upon one!"

"Me?" he laughed. "I am no secret. I am a god in disgrace. Exiled."

"We are brothers, then," I said. "For I, too, am an exile."

"It is different for you," Neptune replied. "You still have your love; that is all that matters."

"If only that were true," I said. "But Isabella left me for another. Perhaps if I can find something to appease her. Something to make her believe in me again."

"You are wasting your time," Neptune repeated. "What's done cannot be undone. You must learn to accept your fate. As I have learned to accept mine."

"No—" I protested.

But he would hear no more. He motioned me away. And then he turned once again to face the deep-blue sea.

INTERLUDE

GODS AND GODDESSES

I t is time to talk about the gods and goddesses. I've referred to them for some time and it must be apparent by now that they are the source of my instability.

I say to myself: I am Franz Herbert. At this instant in time, I am he. And I become me. I enter a state of consciousness where I am no longer cognizant of my corporeal body. I am one of the offspring of the celestial beings who govern the cosmos.

Being an image of these deities, I aspire to know all there is to know. What I am now (this I know), where I came from (this I think I know) and where I shall go (this I know I do not know).

I must not hesitate or falter. And when my search concludes—as one day it must—I shall die. I shall either have attained knowledge and die a saint or have learned nothing and die an idiot.

Which shall it be?

I have seen (I thought I have seen) the gods and goddesses in the center of a distant Galaxy. I have seen (I thought I have seen) the gods and goddesses in the midst of a misty nebula. I have seen (I thought I have seen) the gods and goddesses astride a hidden planet. I have seen (I thought I have seen) the gods and goddesses filling the void that is interstellar space. I have seen (I thought I have seen) the gods and goddesses in a shining constellation. Only I have not seen the gods and the goddesses, I have seen only their shadows. I have not seen eternal light, I have seen only flickering candles. I have not seen that which I thought I have seen.

Is it easy to talk about what the gods and goddesses are not, but this is unsatisfying. So I try another approach: what *are* they?

They are planets. Single points of Being.

They are constellations. Collections of celestial beacons.

They are nebulae. Nebulous clouds of gas and dust.

They are pulsars. The pulse of Existence.

They are galaxies. Or rather, an infinitude of galaxies.

They are supernovae. Celestial fireballs.

They are quasars. Existing at the time of creation.

They are interstellar space. The space between all things.

PART TWO

URANUS

(August 31, 1949)

I have always held a special fondness in my heart for the planet Uranus. It was the first planet discovered in modern times, by the astronomer William Herschel while he was systematically searching the heavens with his telescope on March 13, 1781. He named it Georgium Sidus —the Georgian Planet—in honor of King George III of England. Others called it Herschel in honor of its discoverer. The name Uranus was proposed by the German astronomer Johann Bode in 1803. It became the official name in 1850. Uranus is two billion miles from the Sun. Its discovery doubled the size of the solar system.

Uranus is a giant, blue sphere rising before my eyes as I zero in. Soon it fills my entire viewing screen, a great watery-looking planet with no distinctive features. The planet has no core so I fly right in. The surface is swept by winds that move along at three hundred miles per hour. Seen from the inside I note that Uranus has many interesting cloud features; they range from small to large, from dim and diffuse to sharp and bright, from rapidly evolving systems to stable features that have probably lasted for millennia. There is a long, narrow complex of clouds that is the largest group of atmospheric features I have seen on a planet. I spotted it in the northern hemisphere; it is eighteen thousand miles long!

Uranus is a peculiar planet in several respects. The other planets spin on an axis nearly perpendicular to the plane of the ecliptic, but Uranus' axis is parallel to the ecliptic. This results in a disorienting experience. You feel as though you are trapped in time since the amount of sunlight you receive changes very slowly. A Uranian day lasts approximately forty-two Earth years, followed by a Uranian night of equal duration. Of course that doesn't really matter. You could not breathe on Uranus because its atmosphere is poisonous. And you couldn't stand on the surface because there isn't one. Instead, the atmosphere simply gets thicker and thicker, until it changes from gas to liquid.

Uranus has gigantic hurricanes that last for decades. But the planet, which is nineteen times as far from the Sun as Earth, has far less solar energy to dissipate and therefore these storms are not violent. They swirl and swirl. The storms last so long because the atmosphere has little resistance to help them disperse energy. Uranus really is a peaceful world.

Actually there is a core and it is three times as massive as Earth, but it lies deep below an ocean of ammonia, methane, hydrogen, and helium. A primordial soup. I did not bring my diving suit and so I am unable to investigate. Maybe Isabella—if she ever returns—and I will come here some day and descend to the depths.

On my way home I fly over the five major Uranian moons (there are dozens in all): Miranda, Ariel, Umbriel, Titania, and Oberon. Miranda has giant cliffs, grooves, gullies and other features a lot like you might find in the American West, although much larger; it is only three hundred miles in diameter but has a cliff that is taller than Mount Everest! Ariel is much larger, measuring in at 720 miles; it is heavily cratered and is crisscrossed by groves that look like frozen molasses. Umbriel is the same size as Ariel but the resemblance ends there; it is a very plain place; I spy only one crater; it is shallow and uninteresting. Titania is the largest Uranian moon, nearly 980 miles in diameter. It is made up of rocks and ice, and has lots of ridges, gullies and other features that look like erosion features. Oberon is the last moon I come upon this day. It is slightly smaller than Titania and is almost entirely covered by impact craters. Off in the distance I make out what appears to be a mountain rising from the surface. I train my scientific instruments upon it and discover that it is over three miles high. It is the most interesting feature on the surface.

I realize how much I love it out here in the vastness of space. I could live here forever and not miss a thing back on Earth. All I need is Isabella and the stars. And Pluto, of course, but that goes without saying.

VIII

HOME ON THE RANGE

I returned to Peoria in the fall of 1949. A broken man. So many emotions. Hopelessness, anger, jealousy, despair. Without Isabella, what was there to live for?

I bought a home on the outskirts of Peoria with money I'd saved from my time on the lecture circuit. Then I set about constructing a telescope. With plans adopted from an article in *Sky & Telescope* (a magazine founded at Harvard in 1941), I put together a twelve-inch reflecting scope which I placed atop an equatorial mount. At night I would go out into the cornfields and look up at the heavens.

* * *

A transit of Venus occurs when the planet crosses the disk of the Sun. It moves from left to right across that star's fiery face. It resembles a small, black dot perfectly spherical in nature except when it first crosses and then exits the solar surface; then it takes the shape of a slightly elongated black drop, this due to the effect of the Venusian atmosphere. But it is its insignificance (relative to the significance of the Sun) that amazes me. A speck of dust on the eye of the Solar System.

The ancient Greeks thought that Venus was two objects: a morning star, which they called Phosphorus, and an evening star called Hesperus. In the fourth century BC, Pythagoras realized they were in fact the same object which he termed Venus, the Planet of Love. Johannes Kepler was the first to predict a transit on December 7, 1631. Unfortunately, it was not observed because clouds covered Europe on that day.

Jeremiah Horrocks made the first recorded observation of a transit in 1639. Actually Horrocks was lucky to view the transit for the clouds parted a mere thirty minutes before the it commenced. He observed the transit for nearly four hours making detailed observations that allowed him to estimate the size of the planet and its distance from the Sun.

Horrocks was twenty-one years old at the time. He died suddenly the following year, shot through the heart in a duel over a woman whom both he and another man loved.

Transits are rare, having occurred since then in 1761, 1769, 1874, and 1882. The next transits are in 2004 and 2012 and then again in 2117 and 2125. Do you see the pattern? Venusian transits occur at the following intervals: 121 1/2, 8, 105 1/2, 8, that is they occur in pairs that are eight years apart, the entire pattern repeating every 243 years. The pattern repeats at this interval because 243 orbits of the Earth equals 395 orbits of Venus, that is after this time both planets will have returned to the same point in their respective orbits.

The year is 1949. When the next transit occurs I would be ninety-eight years old. I am sad for in all likelihood I shall not live to see a transit of Venus.

* * *

My new psychiatrist doesn't think I'm crazy. Rather, he encourages me to continue my cosmological endeavors and to attend the meetings of the Peoria Astronomical Society. There, he said, I would find an audience favorable to my way of thinking. I agreed with him. With many celestial observations out here on the plain, there was much I could share.

I was greeted at the society warmly. They knew I had discovered Pluto and were intrigued when I told them how I had gone on to conquer space and time.

The society was an interesting mix of people. There was Fred Tildon, the president, and Joyce White, vice-president. Fred was an amateur astronomer with decades of experience scouring the heavens with a fourteen-inch scope he'd built himself. Joyce was an expert in astrophotography; she enjoyed shooting Earth's moon and the planets. Then there was Ralph Kind, the "comet hunter." He had bagged hundreds over the course of his observing career.

One day, I was asked to deliver a series of talks, reminisces if you will, on the cosmos. Places I had seen and observations I had made. At first I was reluctant. I remembered all too well the ridicule I'd endured at Harvard, and even though years had passed, I found myself growing nervous at the thought of speaking once again before a group.

I told them I'd see what I could put together, but it was months before I felt comfortable enough to do so. It was wonderful, though, to be surrounded by people who had an interest similar to mine.

The society consisted of about fifty members, though no more than two dozen regularly attended. The meetings were held once a month in the auditorium of an old church in downtown Peoria. They followed a standard format. First, a reading of the minutes of the previous month's meeting. Then Sue Kimble talked about principle observing events for the month. Finally, the main event: a lecture by a noted authority on an astronomical topic.

I must be sure to tell Dr. Arnold how grateful I am for his suggestion to attend.

* * *

I have always been fond of galactic structures named after animals. I am perhaps fondest of the Pelican Nebula.

The Pelican Nebula is a large but extremely faint nebula about two thousand light-years away in the northern end of the constellation Cygnus, the Swan. It could hardly have been named anything else for it really *does* look like a swan. It is about thirty light-years wide, surrounded by a dust cloud known as an ionization front which defines the structure's impressive form. Filaments of cold gas—the cosmic feathers—are visible along the front. Within the nebula, dust clouds delineate the eye and the long bill, while a bright front of ionized gas suggests the curved shape of the head and neck. It looks like a playful, young bird. And it is, really, when I gaze upon it.

It is within these dust clouds that star formation occurs. Occasionally jets of hot gas ejected by young stars burst forth like cosmic flares. These flares join and form outflows of plasma or shock waves. They are much like lava flows on Earth. I feel a sense of wonder and awe.

I often travel to the Pelican Nebula on Sunday afternoons. There a plethora of other animals await. They seem to adore me. (They are lonely, I suppose, and enjoy the companionship I bring.) We have fun putting on carnivals. Here comes the zebra, the ostrich, and the giraffe!

Alas, the Pelican is dying. Light from young, energetic stars is slowly transforming the cold gas to hot gas, advancing the ionization front and changing its shape forever. Who knows what it will be called in a million years, the

Elephant Nebula or the Thunderhead or perhaps simply the Blob?

$$* * *$$

In the spring of 1953, I found part-time employment at the Peoria Public Library on Monroe Street. My work involved checking out books and shelf-reading. And I put out magazines. The library subscribed to several scientific magazines—*Scientific American*, *Sky & Telescope*, *Physics Today*—and this let me keep up on the latest developments.

One day I read an article on the recessional velocity of the galaxies. It had been known since the late 1920's—around the time I discovered Pluto—that the distance to a galaxy was proportional to its recessional velocity. Edwin Hubble stated it as follows: $D = V/H$, where D is the distance to the galaxy, V is the galaxy's velocity, and H is a constant (Hubble's Constant).

Note that this depends on a theory (which predicts the value of Hubble's Constant) and observation (determining a galaxy's velocity), either one of which, or both, could be wrong.

And they often were, as I knew from the time I spent investigating galactic distances at Harvard.

I trained my telescope on some of the more exotic galaxies: the Black Eye Galaxy (a dark band of dust partially obscures the galaxy's core), Mayall's Object (which turned out to be two galaxies colliding), and the Tadpole Galaxy (looking like its namesake, it was the result of interaction with a second galaxy which passed nearby).

In truth, my time at the Peoria Public Library was as boring as could be, and as the days dragged on, I found myself disappearing into the cosmos for longer and longer periods of time. By now I had worked at the library seven years. I had the freedom to come and go as I pleased.

* * *

The edge of the universe is a strange place. For one thing, it doesn't exist. At least not like you or I experience existence. At the edge of the universe there is no time or space, for those concepts have no meaning where nothing is. The universe is infinite and, being infinite, it has no center. Where, then, lies the edge? The edge that doesn't exist.

I must travel, then, to the edge that doesn't exist. In my spaceship, I must go. And when I reach the place where the edge should be, I find that it is not. I see that the heavens stretch to the horizon and beyond. There is no alternative but to repeat the process, and this is what I do.

After what seems an eternity, I find the place where the edge must be. It is a line of apparently limitless extent separating that which is from that which is not. I fly around it in my spaceship, study it, if you will, from each one of three hundred and sixty degrees, circumscribing that ray of demarcation, making it the center of its own universe.

I rejoice in the success of my quest—until I realize what a fool I have been. The edge of the universe? I have found nothing of the sort! It was merely a marker. For the next expanse.

The edge of the universe is as illusive as can be. It is there—I know it—but it is not there today. Nothing I can do but soldier on.

* * *

It was the seventh of April, 1962. My attendance at the society had decreased in recent years—my celestial travels were taking up almost all my time—but I recall a stranger who appeared at that meeting.

He was a tall, thin man, with dark-brown hair and large black eyes. A thick mustache. I was sitting in the back of the lecture hall, as I was wont to do. At one point he turned to me and asked my name.

"Franz Herbert," I replied.

"You're the man I've heard so much about."

I asked what he meant.

"The man who discovered the outer planet of our solar system," he said. "The man with an encyclopedic knowledge of the cosmos."

I smiled. "The former is well-known, it's true," I said. "As for the latter . . ." I smiled.

He said his name was Martin Pasqual and that he taught English at the University of Illinois. Astronomy was a hobby of his. He enjoyed going out onto the prairie with his wife and young children and gazing at the heavens.

"I know what you mean," I said. "Nothing compares."

The meeting began—there was a lecture on the geography of Titan by someone whose name I don't recall—but when it had concluded, Pasqual asked if we might continue our conversation, perhaps at a local bar. He was writing an article on Greek and Roman philosophies of the Heavens and would have loved to hear my thoughts.

"Unfortunately I'm not free this evening," I said. "I must be someplace else."

I left it at that.

I did see Pasqual again, later that winter. There must have been a foot of snow on the ground, and I'd retreated to an Irish pub on Water Street one evening after dinner. I remember the bitter cold and a strong northeast wind that was blowing.

I was seated at a table, drink in hand, writing up the details of my latest trip when I heard my name.

It was Pasqual.

He pulled up a chair and told me his article on the constellations had been accepted by the journal *Classical World*. Would I be interested in reviewing the manuscript before he sent off the final version?

I was happy to oblige. I found the article superb; it covered the topic in depth and provided insights into the ancients' state of mind concerning the cosmos. I congratulated Pasqual on its acceptance.

We talked awhile longer—he had several questions about the discovery of Pluto and how it had influenced my career—and when we were done, he thanked me for my time.

Hopefully Martin Pasqual's article was well-received. He was an interesting man. Though our time together had been brief, I felt as if I'd encountered a kindred spirit.

* * *

Pluto is an icy planet. It is about three billion miles from Earth. It is small, smaller than Earth's moon, and it has a moon of its own which is smaller still. The planet's atmosphere is its most amazing feature: it consists primarily of nitrogen and methane, but it exists only when Pluto is closest to the Sun; when the planet moves away the atmosphere condenses and falls back to the planet's surface as frost. Imagine that: one day you can breathe and the next day you can't! This explains why there is no life on Pluto's surface, though it is possible that any life which did exist adapted by moving underground, as it did on Mars.

This celestial iceball is tilted on its axis. When you are on the surface you are dizzy and you will fall quite often. I fall quite often when I am on Pluto. I can't take a dozen steps without falling.

What can I say about Pluto that has not been said a thousand times about other planetary bodies? It orbits the

Sun. It spins on its axis. It is cratered. It is cold. It is dead. But there are secrets about Pluto only I know—and that I will never reveal. And why should I—why should I reveal them? Everyone is entitled to their own private corner of the universe. And Pluto is mine.

* * *

I have been working too hard so I decide to take a trip. Not to the outer reaches of the solar system or anywhere else in space. No, I decide to take an ordinary trip. A road trip. And so I hop into my car and head due east on Highway 74. My destination is Chicago by way of Interstates 74 and 55. I will see the Art Institute of Chicago and the Museum of Science and Industry and of course no trip would be complete without a visit to the Adler Planetarium.

It is an uneventful journey. Uneventful, that is, until I approach Kankakee, about sixty miles from my destination. First I hear the sonic boom. I look up but see nothing. It was only a plane, I think. Moments later I feel inordinate pressure against my eardrums. I hear a whoosh and my body is thrust back into the car seat. And then the unthinkable occurs. From out of the sky a scorching fireball—a fiery meteor—strikes the rear of my car and explodes into a dozen fragments. I smell gas from the punctured gas tank. Seconds later I hear the wail of a police siren in the distance.

It became known as the Kankakee Meteor of 1963. An H6 Chondrite weighing just over twenty-seven pounds. It was first seen over Mississippi as it traveled 634 miles in a northerly trajectory that lasted a mere fifty seconds. Witnesses said the fireball had a greenish tinge, flickered constantly, and produced at least two short-lived flares. Near Memphis, Tennessee a family traveling north on Highway

51 heard what they described as "crackling sounds like a sparkler" as the meteor passed overhead.

Subsequent analysis showed that the meteorite was thirty-two million years old. It was composed mainly of iron and magnesium. It had superheated as it hurtled through the earth's atmosphere, metamorphosing into bizarre shapes that resembled various barnyard animals: pigs, chickens, and cows.

That is, until the meteorite crushed the trunk of my Chevy Malibu and exploded.

I shake my head in dismay.

I tried to escape the Heavens—only for the weekend, mind you!—but it would not let me go.

* * *

The Coma cluster is a rich galaxy cluster. It is in the constellation Coma Berenices. Over the next six months I began a study of the galaxies in the cluster. I catalogued hundreds, including spirals, ellipticals, lenticulars, and irregulars.

An interesting relationship exists between galaxies, quasars, and black holes. A quasar is the very bright centroid of a distant galaxy. It is powered by radiation released from the black hole in the galaxy's center. Quasars are the oldest, most distant objects in the universe. Because they are so far away and so bright we see only the nucleus of the quasar, not the surrounding stars the quasar contains. It is these stars which feed the black hole at the quasar's center, resulting in the emission of radiation which powers the quasar.

When that galactic material is used up the quasar burns itself out; only the black hole remains—the black hole and stars far from the center which aren't sucked into the hole. It resembles a ring galaxy on a supermassive scale.

Is it possible that the Milky Way was quasar-like once and that we are all that remains?

I experience an uneasy feeling. I am at the threshold of a discovery of cosmic proportions. I know it (the concept), only I can not grasp it (the concept's meaning). There is nothing more frustrating than being ever so close to an eternal truth. One may as well be a million light-years away for all the good it will do you.

* * *

The Ancients View the Heavens

a review by Franz Herbert as published in the newsletter of the Peoria Astronomical Society, April 10, 1963

What did the ancients see when they looked at the heavens? Not what you or I see, that much is known for certain. In his article, "The Ancients View the Heavens," published in the March edition of *Classical World*, Dr. Martin Pasqual points out that in ancient times the order of the planets was not what we know it is today. Far from it! The original order of the planets, as set forth by Ptolemy, was as follows: the Moon, Mercury, Venus, the Sun, Mars, Jupiter, and Saturn. Followed by the fixed stars. They believed the stars were fixed because they formed unchanging shapes as placed in the Heavens by the gods.

We laugh at this today, Pasqual writes, but why?

The ancients used the apparent position of these celestial objects to steer their ships by. As Homer sang long ago, "Glorious Odysseus, happy with the wind, spread sails and took his seat with the steering oar as he kept his eye on the Pleiades and the Bootes and the Bear, and he was never plunged in the Ocean, for Calypso had told him to make his way over the sea, keeping the Bear on his left hand."

We smile at this today, Pasqual points out, but why?

The ancients thought that the sky was a semicircular metal firmament surrounding a flat Earth which was itself surrounded by water. The stars were candles stuck in the dome of the sky. Such a structure was, of course, immutable. And thus were the days immutable. Yet the passage of time was governed by the whims of the gods. These mystics concluded that it was the clash between the immutability of the scaffold of life and the whimsical nature of the flesh of life that brought to life its unpredictability, that is, human thoughts and emotions were the consequence of an interaction between the immutability of physics and the whimsy of the gods. It was a cosmic dance that governed life.

We scoff at this today, Pasqual says, but why?

The doctor's point is one we should ponder: what we take to be fiction (the ancient's view of the universe), once was considered fact. Likewise, is it not also true—or probable—that what we take as fact today may one day turn out to be fiction? And if that is the case, is it not also true that this may forever be the case, that is, that we are condemned to exist in a world we will never fully comprehend?

Salient points, Dr. Pasqual, and sobering thoughts.

* * *

The asteroid Toutatis was discovered by French astronomers on February 10, 1934. The asteroid is small, about 2.9 miles long and 1.5 miles wide. Its orbit around the Sun takes four-years and extends from just inside Earth's orbit to the main asteroid belt between Mars and Jupiter.

Toutatis is quite possibly the most bizarre object in the Solar System. It spins like a wobbling football as it hurtles through space It has no fixed axis around which it rotates and thus the concept of a day on Toutatis is meaningless. In fact, its motion is so strange that its orientation with respect to the solar system never repeats. Stars seen from the asteroid appear to crisscross the sky in paths that are always changing. One is literally never in the same place twice and it was this feature of the object that most attracted me. A visit was in order!

It was discovered thirty years ago, as I mentioned, but it quickly disappeared and was considered lost—subsequent observations turned up nothing. And that was where I came in. Finding Toutatis proved to be difficult. Since it has no definite path, my planetary charts were of no help. I circled the Sun several times looking for the elusive body, but it was in vain. It was like the proverbial search for a needle in a haystack. I was at the point of giving up when I noticed a speck of light moving erratically. I figured it was a piece of space debris and I maneuvered my ship to avoid it. But it grew ever closer until I saw it clearly: a dumbbell careening through space. I do not say that I found Toutatis. I prefer to say that Toutatis found me.

I tried to land on the asteroid but failed in the attempt. I descended to several hundred feet above the surface—watched in fascination as the pockmarked surface came into view—but eventually I had to abandon the quest. It was simply too dangerous. What I saw on my approach was interesting, however. Two half-mile wide craters and several prominent ridges. A deep channel that seemed to separate the asteroid into two lobes. My engines were kicking up mountains of asteroid dust that was a powdery gray, and I realized that it threatened to suffocate my ship. What a horrible death that would have been. To die in outer space on a rock that was spinning madly out of control. Even today I shudder at the thought.

DARK MATTER

(October 18, 1963)

Astronomers used to believe that the universe was composed entirely of matter which could be seen: stars, galaxies, nebulae, etc . . . Recently it has been determined that there is more mass in the universe than is directly observable. This extra matter is known as Dark Matter.

Dark matter is matter which emits no light. It is known that this type of matter is the norm, comprising ninety-five percent of the matter in the universe. The problem becomes one of detection: how can astronomers find what they cannot see? The first candidates were burnt-out stars, rogue planets, and black holes. Unfortunately, there are not enough of them to account for the missing ninety-five percent; in fact, they make up only twenty percent of the missing matter.

The remainder consists of a new form of matter composed of entities called non-baryonic particles. These particles are subatomic. Since they are small and account for seventy-five percent of the dark matter there must be a lot of them. So many in fact that they outnumber ordinary matter nineteen to one.

These non-baryonic particles pass through ordinary matter all the time. They are passing through me right now. They are passing through you right now. Generally, they don't interact with ordinary matter, so they are difficult to detect. But they are not undetectable, for occasionally they do interact. What happened when Einstein formulated his theories of relativity was the result of baryonic/non-baryonic interactions. What happened when Mozart composed his symphonies was the result of baryonic/non-baryonic interactions. What happens when I am having an epileptic seizure is the result of baryonic/non-baryonic interactions. In effect, non-baryonic particles comprise a parallel universe that occasionally intrudes upon our own.

The Copernican revolution stated that we are not the center of the universe. It caused quite a stir in its day. Ah, but dark matter presents us with an even more perplexing conundrum. We now know that not only are we not the center of the universe, but that the matter which composes us is exceedingly rare. The vast majority of the universe passes by without paying attention to our existence. We could disappear and it wouldn't notice or even care.

IX

NEW METHODS OF SPACE TRAVEL

One day I started thinking about using black holes to go from one place to another. The science involved was beyond me, but there was one thing I did know: if I tried to travel through a black hole I would surely be ripped to shreds! Might there be a way to avoid this cosmic disintegration?

In any event, my own method of travel was simpler: I think and I go, and I am there.

Dr. Arnold helped me keep my life together when I moved back to Peoria. Though he offered a sympathetic ear, I was discrete about my travels. I still had "visions"—that was the word I used when describing my celestial visitations—but as far as he was concerned they were due to electrical discharges in my brain, perturbations caused by a chemical imbalance in the synaptic structures.

I listened patiently to his theories and took up his prescriptions with a smile. Prescriptions which I never filled, for they might alleviate my condition. My ability to traverse the cosmos would wane and that would never do. So many cosmic wonders beckoned.

One time I mentioned my theory that one might be able to use a black hole to visit the stars.

"My, my, Franz," he said. "You do have a vivid imagination."

He thought I was joking.

I did not correct him.

* * *

How to describe a void—for that is the region of space in which I find myself. It is pitch-black like the bottom of a witch's cauldron, and empty—as far as my eyes can see I spy not a single atom. It is a lonely place, a desolate place, not a kind place, and with no up or down it is disorienting.

The void I am within is five hundred light years across and is located ten billion light years from Earth. When I say there is nothing here, I mean it literally. No stars, no galaxies, no gas, no matter at all, no energy. Nothing but emptiness.

It is a type of emptiness I have never experienced. I cry out in despair—or rather I attempt to do so—but there is nothing in this primitive space to transmit the sound waves of my voice and so I mouth only silence.

I stay in this state for a hundred years.

At this point I notice that my arms are lighter than normal. It is almost imperceptible, but they are my arms, after all, and I know when something is amiss. I see the blackness of space where the flesh of my arms should be. And so it is with my other appendages, my legs, my feet, my hands, and even my torso. I seem to be evaporating. I wonder if it is the effect of the space I am in?

I close my eyes and another hundred years pass.

My mind is here and it is not here. My thoughts are here and they are not here. It's like the time when I was walking down Third Avenue in Las Cruces with Isabella. She was holding my arm, for I was trembling. I remember a torrid sun overhead, its rays a blinding, white light. The buildings that surrounded us were tilted at impossible angles. Isabella, too, looked strange: her face elongated, her eyes open wide as if in fright. I felt as if I was on the borderline. The borderline between what is and what will never be. And then what I was afraid might happen happened: a seizure was upon me and my mind went blank.

So now, Isabella, I must depart this void. Quickly! quickly! I must leave. Or else I will merge with the emptiness, with the nothingness, and myself become empty, become nothing.

* * *

Life went on uneventfully for the next several years. My expenses were minimal and I still had plenty of money from my fame and fortune years. I quit my job at the library in the winter of 1963 so that I could devote my time to celestial travels. When I was back on Earth, I hid myself away at Bradley University's physics library and read up on proposed methods of space travel throughout the ages.

The earliest mention I found was from an ancient Greek writer named Lucian of Samosata in the second century A.D. *True History* described a voyage to the moon and then around the sun and on to distant lands. A small wooden boat was used to traverse the interplanetary medium. It was all quite fantastical, of course, but not more so, really, than what I have accomplished.

The first realistic depiction of space travel was by the Russian science fiction writer Konstantin Tsiolkovsky in 1904. *The Exploration of Outer Space by Means of Rocket Devices* was a theoretical text that discussed the possibility of using a multistage rocket fueled by liquid oxygen and liquid hydrogen. He coined the term "escape velocity," writing that a rocket reaching such a velocity would be free to explore the solar system.

Ridiculed and ignored in his day—as I am in mine—I wonder if, perhaps, Tsiolkovsky and I were brothers, separated not by time, but by space.

* * *

Comets from the Kuiper belt visit our solar system every hundred years or so. Halley's comet is the best-known and brightest of these. It was observed in 1531 and then again in 1607 and again in 1682. It was Edmund Halley who concluded that all three were sightings of the same object: a comet with a period of seventy-six years. He predicted it would return in 1757. Unfortunately, he died in 1742 and did not witness the return of the comet on Christmas Eve in 1758 (having been held up for a year by the gravitational attraction of Jupiter and Saturn).

At this time astronomers scoured the historical records looking for other recorded sightings of this object. There were many. 1059 BC on the occasion of the murder of the Patriarch of Constantinople. 240 BC when the Carthaginian battles were raging. 11 BC when it was known as the Star of Bethlehem. 837 AD when it nearly struck (and would have destroyed) the earth. 1066 AD right before the Battle of Hastings, an event recorded on the famous Bayeux Tapestry. Its most famous appearance, however, was in 1456 when its majestic tail filled the sky, a tail which took on the form of a saber. More recently, visits in 1835 and 1910 correspond to the birth and death of the American novelist Mark Twain.

The orbit of Halley's Comet is, like all comets, highly eccentric. It is inclined eighteen degrees to the ecliptic and has a retrograde motion. The nucleus of the comet is very dark, darker than pitch, darker than coal. It's rather porous, too, like an enormous slush ball.

And it is atop the nucleus that I sit. Riding this colossus through the solar system as it approaches the orbit of Neptune. I howl at the heavens above, at hell below. My eyes glow red like fire. Before me I see the blackness of space. Behind, dusty debris cast off from the comet as it hurtles through space.

Most of these meteors burn up in Earth's atmosphere, but a few make it to the surface. I wonder if any of these particles may have stuck my brain and triggered my epilepsy. A cosmic mutation, as it were, that changed my life forever. It would explain much, perhaps everything.

* * *

While studying at the library, I developed what I call the Herbert Scale of Space Travel. I based it on the ability of a civilization to harness the energy of its environment. I defined four civilization types:

Type One civilizations are able to harness power on a planet-wide scale. They can harvest and store energy reaching their planet from a neighboring star. Power sources are limited to the planet's natural resources and include nuclear fusion, antimatter reactions, and the conversion of one hundred percent of the star's light into electricity.

Type Two civilizations can tap into the power source of their star, transferring the entire energy of the star to storage and distribution centers. Methods include surrounding the star with a storage medium or tapping directly into the star's fusion process.

Type Three civilizations harness the power of their galaxy by controlling the supermassive black hole that exists at the center.

Type Four civilizations are able to harness the power of the universe. They manipulate space-time and travel throughout the universe at will.

Could there be other types as well? Perhaps. I could imagine a Type Five civilization able to harness the power of multiple universes. Its inhabitants would be akin to gods. And maybe a Type Six. That civilization would consist of a single individual. An entity who ruled over Existence. It would be impossible to detect and would appear before us only if it wished to.

Sadly, Earth is not even on the Herbert scale. I guess you could call us a Type Zero civilization, our energy being derived from dead plants.

* * *

The solar wind streams off the Sun in all directions at speeds of about one million miles per hour. The source of the wind is the Sun's corona. The temperature of the corona is so high even the Sun's gravity cannot hold on to it, and it floods the solar system.

The solar wind is not uniform. There are high-speed winds that travel at nearly two million miles per hour and low-speed winds that crawl along at a mere 500,000 miles per hour. There are dense winds and sparse winds. It is the interaction of these winds that produces such phenomenon as auroras and magnetic storms. The solar wind is like a many-layered blanket that envelopes the planets.

As the solar wind expands, its density decreases as the inverse of the square of its distance from the Sun. At a point known as the heliopause, it slows down to a speed of perhaps twenty miles per hour. It is here that the vacuum of space begins.

It turns out there is another wind, a cosmic wind. I came upon it accidentally the first time I ventured out of the solar system. I was floating through the void simply minding my own business and there it was. It gently moved my spaceship from side to side and there was an almost imperceptible increase in acceleration. To tell the truth I thought I might have imagined it, this new wind, but my instruments confirmed its presence.

I have no idea what causes this cosmic wind, but it is a wind I hope to harness to travel between the galaxies. I will use it one day to travel to Andromeda.

$$* * *$$

Dr. Arnold seems interested in my theory of civilization types. He asks me to elaborate. Do I really believe that other civilizations exist?

Most certainly, I tell him. In fact, the probability is a near certainty.

Accepting that to be the case, he said, could we travel to these civilizations—given the bounds of time and space?

All that's needed is the right fuel, I maintain, which is dependent on the civilization type. For a Type Two civilization it would be feasible, for a Type Three it would be child's play.

Dr. Arnold nods. A Peoria Astronomical Society talk would appear to be in order, he said. Perhaps a scientific paper would even result.

I hadn't thought of that, I replied. Why, it might restore my standing in the scientific community!

The session was up and I left, promising the doctor that I would schedule a talk with the society as soon as possible.

But the more I think of it, the less I'm inclined to do so. I was shunned at Harvard. I don't care about those people anymore.

* * *

M104, the Sombrero Galaxy was discovered in 1781 by Pierre Méchain. The name of the galaxy comes from its uncanny resemblance to the broad-brimmed and high-topped Mexican hat. It is located fifty million light years from Earth and is approximately 100,000 light years in diameter. Its mass is about 800 billion suns.

You need a telescope to see the Sombrero from Earth, but it is well worth the effort. It is about one-fifth the size of the full moon, a faint nebula-like object. There is something endearing, almost seductive, about it.

Ah, but M104 is leaving us. At the rate of seven hundred miles per second, it is rushing away from Earth. And this is why one evening I charge across the heavens to rendezvous with El Magnificando before it was too late.

The galaxy has a central bulge of brilliant white stars and is surrounded by striking dust lanes. Close inspection shows they are made up of multi-colored filaments whose purpose I do not understand. I maneuver in as close as I dare and see that the filaments are composed of boulders, cosmic ice balls, and other space debris ranging in size from a few inches to several feet. It is much like the material that composes the rings of Saturn though here there is no obvious source. I stare in disbelief: it is almost as if the filaments are *alive*. Giant wisps of cosmic DNA. I want to investigate, but alas I must move on.

In the center of the Sombrero Galaxy is a black hole that is emitting X-rays at a prodigious rate, a steady stream of radiation that is far greater than any I have recorded. Something unusual is going on, and this, I realize, must be the key to the Sombrero's secrets. I know that incredible forces lie at the center of a black hole, and perhaps that provides the answer. I close my eyes and tumble head over heels, faster and faster. I grit my teeth as my body undergoes horrendous compression. There is no way to describe the horror as I realize I will be ripped to shreds. I call out to Isabella, "Come, and while something of me yet remains, touch me. Take my hand while it is a hand, caress my neck while it is a neck, kiss my cheek while it is a cheek, before I am gone forever."

It is all over for you, Franz, I think.

The wink of an eye, that is what it was. In the wink of an eye, I was *there* and then I was *here*. Back in my room on the planet Earth, sleeping soundly.

I pray to the Great Sombrero. It took me places I had only imagined. But not here. Elsewhere. No one shall ever visit the Sombrero for it disappeared from the event horizon of the universe moments after I left. The galaxy is somewhere else now, as I am somewhere else, someplace else, some else else.

* * *

None of this explains how I do what I do, for, as I said, I think and I go and I am there. And perhaps Dr. Arnold is onto something. The human mind is a medium without equal. An organ which enables cosmic re-awakening. That I have tapped into its power is without question. But what does that *mean?*

It means I can tap into the consciousness of the cosmos just as easily as Isabella is able to control the movement of her left hand. And here I enter the realm of the metaphysical. I am convinced that consciousness—cosmic consciousness—spans the universe. It is composed of blobs of sentience connected by invisible fragments, that is, fragments of sentience connecting one galactic entity to another. It is by traveling along these fragments that we can travel through the cosmos. It is what I, unconsciously, have done.

And here is where Dr. Arnold's theory comes in. It is true—it must be true—that electrical perturbations in my brain enable my mind to connect with this cosmic consciousness. That I am aware of what is happening is what puzzles me. It must be related to my epilepsy. A subtle shift in the fabric of my own space. But why me? And why now?

I make a note to discuss this with the doctor. I must be careful not to give myself away. My circumstances, I mean. I will couch the description of my cosmic travels in a language the doctor will find familiar. And less threatening. The language of dreams.

"I've written down the story of a lost constellation," I say at our next meeting. "I thought that by embedding my thoughts it might help you to better understand me."

Dr. Arnold nods. "And you to understand yourself."

"Perhaps . . . Let me read it to you. It's called—"

Ophiuchus

Pity the constellation Ophiuchus. Someone had to go and it was the one.

The Zodiac is the path the Sun, the Moon, and the planets Mercury, Venus, Mars, Jupiter, Saturn, and Uranus cut through the heavens. (Pluto's orbit is so bizarre that it does not follow this path.) Twelve constellations constitute the zodiac, one for each month of the year, though thirteen reside in it. The zodiac was invented by the Babylonians in 1000 BC; it served as an ancient calendar. At that time the Sun did not travel through Ophiuchus and so it was not included. In the second century A.D., the Egyptian astronomer Ptolemy enumerated the modern constellations of the zodiac, but he left out Ophiuchus. It is not known why he did so, for he writes elsewhere of the importance of this constellation. I suppose all he needed were twelve and so one had to go.

The constellations of the zodiac, like all constellations, are not what they appear to be. They are wholly imagined by man. The stars which comprise them are not adjacent in three-dimensional space. That is, if from another region of the galaxy one were to look towards the region of space where we see Orion one would see something else or even nothing at all!

Remember this to recall the constellations of the zodiac:

The Ram, the Bull, the Heavenly Twins,
And next the Crab, the Lion shines,
The Virgin and the Scales.
The Scorpion, Archer, and the Goat,
The Man who holds the Watering Pot,
And Fish with glittering scale,
And poor Ophiuchus, neglected and forgotten.

Ophiuchus, though neglected, is a fascinating constellation. It is depicted in the sky as a man holding a snake. Prominent stars include Rasalhague, near the man's head; Marfik, at the left elbow; and Sabik, on the right leg. In 1604 Ophiuchus hosted Kepler's Supernova, the last supernova observed by mankind for several hundred years. Kepler described it in his book entitled: "On the New Star in Ophiuchus' Foot." Ophiuchus also contains Barnard's Star, one of the snake's "eyes."

Barnard's Star is the second-closest star to Earth at ten light-years distant.

Even though Ophiuchus is not a Zodiacal constellation and Pluto is not a planet (or so many claim) Pluto has been in the constellation Ophiuchus my entire life. This must be why I feel such an affinity for both objects.

The mythology of Ophiuchus is particularly interesting. The great hunter Orion boasted to the gods that he would kill all great beasts on Earth. Since they could never let this happen they sent a serpent to sting Orion on the heel. Orion cursed the gods as he felt his life force fading.

Ophiuchus was a physician who had learned the secrets of life and death from a serpent. He could even bring people back from the dead. He healed Orion on the spot and ground the serpent under his foot. Hades complained to Zeus that the underworld was threatened. So Zeus killed Ophiuchus with a thunderbolt and enshrined him in the Heavens for he realized that he was not really a bad man.

* * *

"Very interesting, Franz," Dr. Arnold says when I finish. "And quite clever. Indeed, I see parallels between Ophiuchus' story and your own."

I nod. "It's clear to me," I say. "People think Ophiuchus is a constellation unworthy of the Zodiac, they think Pluto is a body unworthy of the Planets, and they think I am a man unworthy of the name Astronomer."

* * *

March 10, 1966. In honor of my sexagenarian status, I compose an essay summarizing my time upon the earth. It's a companion piece of sorts to Dr. Pasqual's essay but looking in instead of out. I think I'll call it:

Secrets of Life

I turned sixty the other day, though I feel as if I'm still twenty, lying on my back in the backyard of my parent's home in Peoria with Isabella at my side, looking up at the night sky.

But I am not. I am older. Much older. The universe no longer needs me, for I am no longer fertile. It is preparing to cast me aside.

And yet I have just discovered the secret of life! It was quite unexpected. I had been searching my entire life, searching my entire life for the secret of life, and when my sixth decade was drawing to a close and I seemed no nearer to its divination, I assumed there was no longer any hope. No hope for a man with one foot in the grave.

I was tired of searching and I wanted to spend the remainder of my days staring out the living-room window of my home on the outskirts of Peoria, staring at the birds pecking at the feeders I dutifully filled every Sunday afternoon, gazing upon my flower garden, the garden made in the image of the one I tended when I was a child and that meant more to me than anything in the world.

But at night I searched the heavens in a quest to find something—anything—that might reveal the secret of life. Or that would point the way. Might it appear in the image of a planet? or a constellation? or a star?

When people ask "What is the secret of life?" what they really mean is, "What do I have to do to be happy?" And that is an altogether different question. Happiness means different things to different people. To some it means money—the accumulation of wealth. To these people the secret of life is to play the stock market. One can make vast sums of money in the market, it is true, though one can also lose one's shirt; therefore one must be careful. Even so, with the utmost care the most one will make is eight percent and eight percent is definitely not the secret of life.

Other people couldn't care less about money. To them happiness means love. I don't really want to discuss that most fundamental of human emotions except to say that finding love is nearly impossible. But that won't stop people from spending a lifetime trying. It is sad for inevitably it leads to broken promises, broken homes, broken dreams and if you think I am speaking from experience you are right.

There are those who believe happiness lurks behind rocks. There are those who believe happiness lurks behind doors. There are those who believe happiness lies at the end of the rainbow just after the rain has cleared. There are those who aren't so sure. There are those who believe happiness isn't anywhere at all for it's nothing but an illusion. I myself am an illusion. I became one long ago. About the time you left me for that repairman in Watertown.

If the secret of life is not happiness, what else might it be?

Immortality, says the priest who has taken his vows. To live forever—whether on heaven or on earth—has its attractions, it must be acknowledged. But the search for immortality has driven multitudes into the arms of every crackpot one can imagine: The alchemist who, with a bitter incantation, turns lead into gold. It is an illusion. The gold does not glitter; it is dull, like lead. The clairvoyant who divines in tea leaves at the bottom of the cup that the world is about to end. An illusion. The world is not about to end. It will spin until the Sun explodes and that will not be until you and I are dead and gone. The magician who, with a wave of his hand, levitates the living. Merely an illusion. What one sees is not necessarily what is. A magician is but a thief who picks your pocket.

Fame. Ah, fame. The secret of life is fame. Or so many seem to believe. And it is true that to be known, recognized, and admired is unquestionably a universal desire. Why, fame even comes—in the most severe cases—with its own line of live-action dolls! But the trappings of fame are also well-known. As is the famous one's fate: to become the object of jealousy, ridicule, and scorn. Far better to be a common man swallowed up by the sea of humanity. Or better still, to never have existed. Like I no longer exist. Without you.

There was a woman in Las Cruces who was a ballerina. She talked endlessly of pointes, pirouettes, and the barre. She dreamed that one day she would be famous and dance before adoring crowds. She was a pretty woman and a very talented dancer. But I don't think she could have handled fame. In any event, she never got the chance, for one morning she was killed when crossing the street in front of her apartment. Struck dead by an automobile. She never knew what hit her and it was better that way. Her blood flowed into the street like wine.

There was a woman in Flagstaff who had been so happy once upon a time. But as the years passed her happiness turned into sorrow and eventually she pleaded for mercy at the hands of the man she'd married many years before. She thought he knew the secret of life but all he knew was a blinding rage. He beat her mercilessly, beat her without meaning to beat her for he really loved her you see, like you really loved me once. His cold, tiger-eyes laid waste to her soul.

There was a woman at Harvard who was a writer. She wrote many pieces, a handful of which were published in well-known magazines. But she was never satisfied with anything she wrote. She burned drafts of stories others thought were promising. She berated her husband when creativity would not flow. She would rant and rave for hours on end. The critics said she had writer's block, would never write anything worthwhile again. One day she said, "To hell with everything!" and threw herself out the window. I'll never forget that day, so gray and sad with the mists rising before me.

When I was eighteen, I went to a college out west. I was young and innocent and my head was filled with big ideas. There was a young man on campus who was a singer. He was tall and handsome, his eyes a deep blue, his dark hair long and curly. All the girls adored him. He would play a guitar on the campus quad most evenings and in coffee houses around town on Saturday nights. He sang simple songs about love and faith. He was out to change the world, he said. He was not an angry man, but he was passionate. I always thought he would do great things in life, and many years later I inquired about him. Had he found fame and fortune? Had he managed to change the world? It turned out it was neither. He died tragically one cold winter night in his fortieth year. Shot dead in a tavern in Baltimore. A petty argument over a girl. And I leave it up to you to decide whether he had discovered the secret of life. You who are dead and gone and who exist only in these images my mind has so carefully constructed.

You've had enough of me by now. You think I'm one-off, I know. All right, then. Have it your way. A new day has arrived and I feel as if I am clutching at the air. In my garden, the butterflies hover like sleepwalkers. The scarlet tanager has alighted at the feeder; I haven't seen him in quite some time but I know he knows my secret. You will just have to figure it out for yourself!

TARANTULA NEBULA

(June 19, 1967)

"Bring her in slowly," the captain said. "We don't want any surprises."

The *Saratoga* was a ten-ton vessel, fast and eminently maneuverable, with a propulsion system that was top-of-the-line. It was the first ship to visit the Tarantula Nebula and the crew was well aware of the momentousness of the event.

It had been an eight-month voyage, uneventful, launched from Earth in 3157. The forty-eight crew members were space veterans, having visited among them thirty-six comets, eighty-four asteroids, sixty-two planets, and twelve-star systems.

But this mission was different: the objective was to pilot a vessel into an enormous cloud of gas and dust.

The Tarantula Nebula is located 160,000 light-years from Earth in the Large Magellanic Cloud. The nebula is immense, measuring 650 light-years across at its widest point. A seemingly endless supply of hydrogen gas is the fuel that produces young stars. The nebula's wispy arms resemble a spider's legs.

But none of that mattered, for the men of the *Saratoga* found themselves faced with a phenomenon no one had ever encountered.

Imagine sailing into a black fog thick as tar, and into an electrical storm unlike any ever encountered. The *Saratoga's* instruments registered nothing, that is, nothing sensible. Readings that were either off the scale or non-existent. The first systems to be affected were electronics (scrambled), mechanical (not functioning at all), and biological (life forces slowly ebbing). Eventually, systems stabilized, but by then the ship was operating at minimal power levels. Engineering said that in six hours life support would be critical.

The captain, a man in his early thirties, ordered communications to send a warning message to Mission Control. He realized there was virtually no chance it would get through, but he knew they had to try. Buffeted fore and aft by what his science team suspected were gravitational waves, all they could do was pray.

It was some time later when they emerged from the maelstrom into a blinding white light that dissipated to reveal a spider's lair. The members of this veteran crew, who had seen so many galactic wonders, had stared death in the face countless times without flinching, could do nothing but cry out in despair.

* * *

"That was the final transmission," the mission commander said. "The final *coherent* transmission." There were two others, but neither made sense. The first was frantic, something about being dragged into a whirlpool. And a reference to a web of death and deceit." He stopped and swatted at a fly that had settled on his coffee mug.

"And the second?" the reporter prodded.

The mission commander laughed. "The weirdest of all! I remember the words exactly: 'There really is a tarantula at the heart of the Tarantula Nebula.'" He frowned. "We'll never know what the *Saratoga's* fate was. And perhaps that's a good thing. Perhaps some of the universe's mysteries best remain hidden."

"I'm not sure I agree . . ." the reporter began.

But his words fell on deaf ears, for the commander had turned on his heels and was already halfway down the hallway.

* * *

That was how I imagined it, anyway, as I watched from the confines of my observatory in Peoria, Illinois, my telescope centered on the heart of the nebula. Should I have told the *Saratoga's* crew its fate? Relative to me, they were 160,000 light-years away, but, as I'd recently discovered, information sent on a beam of light would reach them instantaneously. Even so, there was nothing they could do to avoid the end. And so I watched, horror-stricken, as they were devoured by the bulbous arachnid. An arachnid that one day will spawn millions which will themselves spawn millions which will collectively consume the cosmos.

You see, not even I am immune. In the depths of night, under a starry sky, I feel a gentle tug, barely perceptible, but it's there I'm sure. An invisible string that draws me to my death just as it drew the *Saratoga* to hers. And I wonder: is there someone watching me, someone who could warn me of my fate, but who chooses not to do so?

X

I'M STILL HERE!

Skip, skip, skip to my Muse,
Skip, skip, skip to my Muse,
Skip, skip, skip to my Muse,
Skip to my Muse, my darling.

With forty years of celestial travel under my belt, one would have thought I had visited every interesting place in the cosmos. Luckily, that was not the case. Lacking work and family duties I was free to roam, to discover new places and visit old friends. . . .

* * *

Seen through a high-powered telescope the Horsehead Nebula is the most magnificent object in the universe, but it looks even more stunning if you visit in person. And it was on a fair September day that I decided to get away—fourteen hundred light years away—to that sea of gas and dust that lies just south of the bright star Zeta Orionis in the constellation Orion.

Seen from Earth the Horsehead Nebula looks like a dark cloud in the shape of a horse's head, but up close one sees that it is amorphous and glows in various colors, each corresponding to a distinct section of the nebula. Red light from the continual emission of hydrogen atoms silhouettes the nebula like a bogeyman's cape. Brown light, the color of obscuring dust, forms the horse's shape—its neck, head, and mane. Blue-green light is from scattered starlight that appears to come from deep inside the nebula. This last color reminds me of the glow of Earth's oceans as seen from outer space. Could it be that Earth's genesis was similar?

I must fly inside the nebula to determine its origin.

First the horse's neck, a mountain of dust as thick as pea soup. I cannot see a thing and I worry lest my navigational controls malfunction and I find myself adrift in an endless fog. Moments later I enter a clearer region and I see starlight in the distance and the familiar heavens and then I am plunged into the horse's head, an even denser area of total darkness. Finally, the mane, an area in which there is less dust along my line of sight and the background emission from hydrogen atoms can be seen through the surrounding dust.

I am nearly on top of the nebula and it is one of the scariest sights I have ever seen. No longer does it resemble any earthly shape or celestial form ever seen or imagined but is instead a chaotic mass made up of wispy filaments and diffuse dust. And I see that the bright blue-green area beyond the horse's head is really a cosmic oven: a nursery where stars are born. I am blinded by the brilliance of the surrounding starlight, starlight that is blocked from reaching Earth by the very dust that forms the nebula.

* * *

I returned to Peoria and was entering the foyer of my house when who should I come upon but Isabella and Jason sprawled on the couch in the living room!

"Father!" Jason exclaimed.

My beloved son was thirty-eight years old. All grown up with a full head of thick jet-black hair, fiery brown eyes, strong limbs. Even so his face still possessed the innocent look of a child. My child. My Argonaut.

"We've been waiting for you for some time; where have you been?" Isabella scolded. Her angry eyes held me rooted to the spot.

My estranged wife was as beautiful as ever. Her long, black hair tied up in a bun. Her crystal eyes glistening in the pale light of the afternoon sun which was streaming through the bay window.

"I'm sorry," I said. "I returned just now." I told her of my recent adventures.

"How is your . . . condition?" she asked. She always spoke of my epilepsy in this way.

"Stable," I said. "I'm back on medication and my doctor says I'm doing well. Luckily, it hasn't hindered my travels. I'd never forgive him if it did!" I turned to Jason. "And how is my wandering son?" I asked. "Any adventures of your own?"

He told me his own story. Of descending to the underworld and what he found there.

"How wonderful," I said. "Tell me of Orpheus and Eurydice. Did you meet them?" I glanced at Isabella and saw that she was in tears. I went up to her and we embraced. "I've missed you," I said.

"Yes," she whispered. "And now all will be as it was before. . . ."

Of course, none of this actually occurred. The room I walked into was empty.

But that doesn't mean one couldn't imagine it otherwise.

✳ ✳ ✳

The most enchanting objects in the visible universe are quasars. They are the very bright centers of distant galaxies, galactic ovens so bright they drown out the light from all other stars in their galaxy. They are not large, only about three thousand light years in diameter. That is not much larger than the diameter of our own solar system. They form when gas and dust spirals into a supermassive black hole which lies at the center of a galaxy.

The nearest quasar is three billion light years from Earth; so it will take longer to reach my destination than is usual. I hop aboard my spaceship and am off, on a direct heading to 3C 273.

It is not long before I find myself in intergalactic space. I have my viewing screen trained on 3C 273; as it grows steadily closer, I tremble with anticipation.

3C 273 is not only the nearest quasar to Earth, but it is the brightest as well. It has a large active galactic nucleus from which emanates a jet composed of radio waves that travel at roughly the speed of light. As with all quasars, it contains a black hole at the center. This one is particularly active, swallowing matter at a rate of a dozen solar masses per year.

Alas, I never get to my destination, to 3C 273. I am perhaps a thousand light years away—but the quasar speeds up, its rate of acceleration away from my ship matching my rate of acceleration towards it so I get no nearer. What I do observe, from a safe distance, are two galaxies colliding. It is a sight I am fortunate to witness, for occurrences are rare. And it fills me with horror: Galaxy A—the predator—rips the guts out of its victim, Galaxy B, spewing radioactive gas and gaseous clouds for hundreds of light years. I hear the death screams of B's stars as they die. As I will one day die, cast out into the cosmos like a bundle of star dust that has been and will be no more. Detritus.

* * *

It occurs to me, Isabella, that I have never revealed *how* I traverse the cosmos.

I never told you because, well, I was never sure myself.

It was when I was en route to Thor's Helmet, a bubble-shaped nebula in Canis Major, about twelve thousand light years from Earth, that I finally realized what was happening.

Consider: Nothing that travels through space can travel faster than the speed of light, 186,000 miles a second.

Consider: Any particle that travels at the speed of light has no mass.

Consider: Time slows as one approaches the speed of light. Theoretically, if one were to attain the speed of light, time would stop.

Consider: This means that photons—light's massless particles—are aware of all other photons in the universe. For them time is a concept without meaning. For them they are everywhere and everywhere at once.

Therefore, if Franz Herbert could turn himself into a photon, he could be anywhere he wanted. Instantaneously.

That's what an epileptic seizure does to me. It turns me into a photon. Resulting in a sudden transformation. Life with one foot in many places.

How I wish you were here, Isabella, so that I could explain all of this to you. As it is, there is only me and my beloved Pluto. And the silence of these walls.

* * *

The Oort Cloud is one of the most amazing structures in the universe, though I am the only person who has seen it. It is a vast cloud at the edge of the solar system and is the source of many comets. They rain down on our solar system like darts, occasionally striking one of the planets, sometimes with catastrophic consequences. But more often they do not; they are captured by the Sun and orbit forever in periods of millions of years.

The cloud is spherical in shape and contains predominately icy planetesimals, cosmic dust grains that stuck together over time to form larger bodies. It is several billion years old and contains approximately twelve billion comets, the total mass of which equals about forty Earths. It is 900 billion miles in diameter, halfway to the nearest stars. It formed from the collapse of the nebula that formed the Sun and the planets. I think of it as a celestial placenta.

This is all well and good, of course, except that the Oort cloud isn't a cloud at all. It's a machine. A giant cosmic clock. And the comets it generates aren't comets. They are clock ticks. Twelve billion comets. Twelve billion ticks of the clock. And when the last tick has tocked the Oort Cloud will exist no more. Ground into a dust of dust, it will vanish with a sigh.

* * *

I received a letter the other day from Isabella! There was no return address, but the writing was unmistakably hers. Soft and gentle. With tender curves.

She asked how I was and what I was doing. She wished me well. She wrote that she was living in an old farmhouse in Maine and was working on a book. That was all that she said.

She must have contacted Harvard and found out where I'd gone after my dismissal (New Mexico), then traced me to Peoria. I couldn't believe she'd taken the time. What did she want? Had her new relationship floundered? I could only hope it was so.

* * *

A sigh is an apt description of my next encounter. The Crab Nebula is nothing *but* a sigh. A vast supernova remnant, it was created in an explosion that occurred on July 4, 1054, an explosion so huge it was visible in the daytime for twenty-three days and in the night sky for nearly two years. The event was observed all over the world and was recorded by Chinese astronomers and American Indians.

About one hundred years after the explosion the nebula formed. A cloud of gas and dust ten light years in diameter, six hundred light years from Earth. The nebula itself was discovered by Charles Messier in 1758 when he was searching for Halley's comet on its first predicted return. At first he thought it *was* Halley's comet, but subsequent observations convinced him this was not the case. Messier christened it M1 and logged it as the first entry in his catalogue of stellar objects.

The Crab Nebula is beautiful. It is composed of hues of red and blue, fast-moving electrons that both approach Earth (the reds) and recede (the blues). I am struck by how harmonious it seems. I am floating through boundless stretches of gas and dust, lost in a great cosmic expanse. And it strikes me: I am attracted to the Crab Nebula because I *am* the Crab Nebula, that is, like the nebula, I am an entity composed of gas and dust belched from a star long ago.

At the center of the nebula is a pulsar. It rotates thirty times a second. A marvelous chronological machine. I tap-dance as it spins. And I sing a song about birth and death and of love which is everlasting.

* * *

Isabella's second letter bore a return address—Castine, a small coastal town in Maine. She wrote that she would be setting sail from Boston in a month, a ship bound for Italy. She had never been outside the continental United States, had never expressed interest in traveling abroad, so this was quite a shock!

She didn't say why she was going, nor what she would do when she got there or if she was going alone, or, this most important of all, when she might return. But she did ask—thoughtfully, I supposed, perhaps with a bewitching expression as she penned the words—if I would like something from across the sea.

* * *

The Tarantula Nebula was first cataloged as a star, 30 Doradus. It was reclassified as a nebula by the astronomer Abbe Lacaille in 1752. It is more than one thousand light years across and is about 170,000 light years from Earth. Inside this cosmic arachnid lies a central young cluster of massive stars whose intense radiation has helped energize the nebular glow and shape the spidery filaments that shoot outward from the center.

An interesting structure named Hodge 301 is embedded deep within the Tarantula Nebula. Many of the stars in Hodge 301 are so old they have become supernovae. They blast stellar material into the surrounding region at speeds of almost two hundred miles per second. This high-speed matter is plowing into the surrounding regions, compressing the gas into a multitude of sheets and filaments. The tarantula's tentacles. I dare not journey into this place. I fear I would become entangled there. Held in the grip of this spidery creature, I would never be able to return to Earth. To flee that web of death.

You see, there really *is* a tarantula at the center of the Tarantula Nebula. It is a monstrous creature—a living, breathing entity—that rules over the surrounding space. I have seen it from afar. Hairy and shadowy and covered with blood. I shudder as I recall that time.

* * *

The third letter Isabella and I exchanged was mine. I told her that I missed her. That the only thing I wanted was to kiss her lips. Was that too much to ask?

Why did I ask this? Why did I ask this of Isabella? I don't really know! It was crazy, I suppose. *She* left *me*, after all. Maybe I was trying to find out whether she missed me.

Perhaps.

Perhaps.

Perhaps.

Perhaps our love was nothing then. As it is nothing now. Or perhaps it was (and is) everything.

I asked Isabella in closing: When might she return? When might that be?

* * *

As frightening as that journey proved to be, there was another that was even more harrowing. The spiral galaxy M51 is commonly known as the Whirlpool Galaxy. It was discovered by Charles Messier on October 13, 1773. He described it as a large, faint nebula. Its companion galaxy, NGC 5195, was discovered eight years later on March 21, 1781. It looks like a faint, round blob. Lord Rosse made a detailed drawing of the two galaxies in 1845, the larger M51 with its spiral arms on top of a round dot-like galaxy that is NGC 5195. He called it Rosse's Question Mark galaxy. And that's exactly what it looks like!

The Whirlpool Galaxy is a factory. Dark clouds of gas are transformed into stellar furnaces that generate new star clusters. NGC 5195 is not tugging on M51—as Rosse had conjectured. Rather, NGC 5195 is passing *behind* M51, like a freighter that is drifting past a second ship. But it does influence its companion. NGC 5195 is old and massive. As it drifts by M51 it generates radiation waves that pass through M51's gas clouds, causing them to collapse, superheat, and spark the star-building process. It is like the pilot light of a fiery furnace.

The center of M51 is the hottest place in the universe. At least the hottest I have come upon. In an act of total recklessness, I maneuver my spacecraft directly above it and find myself gazing down on a single point of infinite light. Imagine looking into a fire of pure whiteness. A fire so bright it blinds and the whiteness becomes darkness. I was blinded then—though only momentarily. At some point the darkness receded and I saw—no I cannot say the words. It was Horror itself, beyond that I shall not go.

* * *

Isabella was blunt: she wasn't sure if she *was* coming back. It depended on how she was feeling after a year abroad. She'd been doing a lot of thinking, she wrote, and realized she needed a change. Her life was no longer pointing towards the stars as I had said it must do. Did I understand? In any event, this was what she needed.

She would be staying in a cottage in the Italian alps in a region known as the Elf-Child, famous for the circus animals that inhabited the region: the Elephant, the Lion, the Giraffe, and the Bear—so much fun to wander amongst them!—a place covered in snow that rose in drifts that went on for miles. One could easily get lost in those Italian Alps. One could lose one's way and never return.

She concluded with a paragraph that invoked the image of a mirror. A mirror that had been shattered. A mirror she was trying to piece together, but which, she realized, would never be the same. And I wondered: did she mean to call up the paradoxes of continuity and discontinuity which had plagued the ancient Greeks? I had often talked to her about them.

* * *

The Coalsack Nebula is a dense cloud composed of molecular hydrogen which absorbs the light from the stars behind it. It is visible to the naked eye in the Southern Hemisphere and is the most prominent nebula in the sky. It is approximately six hundred light years distant in the constellation Crux.

The British astronomer William Henry Smyth gave it the name "Black Magellanic Cloud" in 1820. He theorized that the Coalsack was not totally black. It had a faint glow (undetectable by the telescopes of that time) that was caused by the emission of light by the stars it obscured.

When I reached the nebula after a three-day journey, I found myself facing what looked like an enormous sack of coal. It was perfectly black (Smyth had been wrong) but there were objects inside, objects which were glowing.

Since the top of the sack was open, I maneuvered my ship and dropped inside. A foolish move, perhaps, but I learned something interesting: the Coalsack Nebula is the Devil's Lair. Beelzebub lives there. I watched as he roasted marshmallows on an open fire. He was laughing, a sonorous belly laugh, a sound as loud as the thunderclaps that echoed from Mount Olympus. And perhaps that's what they were?

* * *

The final letter was from me. If Isabella was not going to return, there was one thing she could send me: an Italian telescope with precision optics, a hand-ground mirror. Then I could gaze at her forever from across the sea. Wouldn't that be grand!

* * *

When I approached 3C 273—this was my second attempt; after adjustments to my ship, I was able to outpace the receding object—I was dazzled by its luminescence, its pulsating lights that seemed to stretch endlessly in all directions.

Alas, but there was nothing in the space surrounding 3C 273, that is, there were no stars, no planets, no galaxies, no nebulae. Simply beacons of light that comprised 3C 273, like the ommatidia of an insect's eye. Some glowed blue, others red, orange, or white. I hovered before them, transfixed.

I took a deep breath and fell head over heels into the quasar. I found it was not one object but an infinite number, an infinite number of mini-quasars that marked the beginning of time and I realized I was about to know what came before time, before existence, and it was at that moment that I grew fearful.

I realized that God lay beyond the quasar and I did not wish to confront Him.

* * *

I've never mentioned my housekeeper, Mrs. Brooks, but there she was dusting the living room furniture when I entered the front door one afternoon in early November.

"Well, dear me, if it isn't Franz Herbert!" she exclaimed.

I smiled. Truth be told, I was exhausted from my travels. I set my suitcase down on the carpet.

"And where have you been this time?" she asked. "It must have been a month since I've seen you."

I smiled again. "Just around . . ." I said. And around and around and around.

I went into the kitchen and fixed myself a drink. When I returned to the living room she was dusting one of the oak bookcases.

Mrs. Brooks was in her late forties. She had short, curly brown hair. Gray eyes. A chubby, round face. I didn't know much about her, only that her husband was an invalid and she cleaned houses to support the two of them. She did an excellent job and was well worth the two hundred dollars I gave her each month.

She had admired my backyard telescope several times. One winter, around seven in the evening—she was just finishing up—I let her look through the lens, up at Jupiter and its four bright moons.

She uttered an expansive sigh. "So beautiful . . . and it makes me wonder . . ." She broke off.

"About the meaning of life," I said, completing her thought. "Is this really all there is?"

"Yes."

I looked up at the celestial sky. "No," I said. "There's more. Much more."

"You're always traveling, Mr. Herbert," she said, "Seeing new people and new places. So you must know: what *is* the meaning of life?"

"The meaning of life is love," I said without hesitation. "And let me tell you why. . . ." I went to my bedroom and returned with two sheets of yellowed notebook paper.

* * *

PKS 1127-145 is a glowing cloud of gas and dust, a huge space bubble surrounding a supermassive black hole which consumes the equivalent of a dozen stars a year. Even as the black hole consumes matter, the quasar throws off an intense wind of electromagnetic energy, the equivalent of three hundred average galaxies. The wind's speed is approximately four million miles an hour. As the quasar expands it pushes the surrounding gas outwards into a shell; the gas is then ionized which causes it to glow. The shell extends at least a million miles from the quasar. I observe beautiful shades of green, red, yellow, and blue. It really does look like an enormous bubble and thus I have dubbed it the Bubble Quasar. The quasar is ten billion light years from Earth and is four light years in diameter. It appears in the constellation Crater.

As I approach I see that the Bubble Quasar is actually a huge bubble network—there are three main bubbles and thousands of smaller ones connected together. I try to penetrate one of the main bubbles but am unable to do so. There is more galactic material to the northeast of the bubble (northeast of where I am); the stellar wind is less intense in that direction and the bubbles are thicker. I go southwest and am able to penetrate one of the smaller bubbles. The interior is filled with a gelatinous substance. My engines sputter and for a moment I fear I will be trapped. Putting the engines in reverse, I make a hasty escape and from a safe distance I observe the bubbles gently pulsating.

The Bubble Quasar reminds me of a gigantic placenta and the thought crosses my mind that maybe that is exactly what it is. Am I witnessing a holy cosmic birth?

* * *

Fare-Thee-Well: An Ode to Isabella

as recited by Franz Herbert
to his housekeeper Mrs. Elaina Brooks
on the eighteenth of November, 1967

I remember how I watched you as you loped across the shore, the wind blowing through your hair. You were not aware that I was watching. You gazed out over the sea as if searching for something you knew you would not find. The truths of Aphrodite were in your eyes, the secrets of Athena, and I realized you were searching for nothing, that the sea was inside of you, and you were simply coming home. It was then I realized I wanted nothing more than to spend my entire life with you—that you were the woman for whom I had been searching. And it was then, I think, I realized we would never love one another, or rather, that you would never love me, for you were like a child wrapped up in a blanket of solitude. I realized this, as I watched you on the shore, but I did not realize it in my heart; and so instead of turning away, which is what I should have done, I hurried towards you, my hand outstretched.

And now our time together has passed. Fare-thee-well. Like an angel of grace you are and I shall love you forever.

* * *

A cosmic birthing place is what lies in the Southern Cross, one of the best-known constellations in the southern hemisphere. It is not visible north of latitude thirty degrees but is visible all year long from latitudes south of thirty-four degrees. The constellation lies along the Milky Way and is surrounded on three sides by Centaurus, the Centaur. It is made up of four bright stars situated at the ends of a cross. Its brightest star is called Acrus and is actually a double-star system. The other stars are named Becrux, Gacrux,

191

and Deka Crucis. The Southern Cross is a small constellation, but it is a radiant jewel in the sky. It was used by mariners in the southern hemisphere to guide their ships.

It is a distant constellation; the stars that comprise it lie between two and six hundred light years away. One of its open clusters is known as the Jewel Box cluster. It is rumored that Zeus lives in this space, directly behind the center of the cross, and because of that I will never go inside. I have hovered around the Jewel Box, though. It is a young cluster with an estimated age of only ten million years. It contains about one hundred stars and is a mere twenty light years across. Most of its stars are blue dwarfs but one of its more prominent is a red supergiant.

It is my belief that the gods and goddesses created the cluster, but for what purpose only they know. Is it simply a place in which to live? A place from which to rule over Heaven and Hell? Or is it something else: a fourth dimension or a fifth or a sixth or the entrance to a pathway that will take you to a seventh?

* * *

I remember when you slept beside me, your strawberry hair across my shoulders. We loved each other for so many years. We raised a son and now he is gone. Vanished like a firefly in the night. But something else vanished, too. It slipped out the door when we weren't looking, did not let us know it was departing. Our love for each other—where did it go, where did it go, my love?

We would have withered and died if we had not found one another, we were always so fond of saying. "Make love to me," you said and I eagerly complied. Ah! Those hot and steamy nights, those dreamy days, when we rushed through life without knowing what we were doing, or where we were going, because we had each other and our love was all that mattered.

How many times have I kissed your tapioca lips, brushed your long silken hair, felt the warmth of your slowly beating heart?

Our love was our compassion, our love was our kindness. But our love was also our anguish and our despair, for each passing moment only brought us closer to that final separation, that yawning abyss of loneliness, that eternal chasm of solitude. That is what our love became. We loved until we could love no longer, until everything we held dear had gone up in smoke, until the gossamer strands of our love were broken, until there was nothing left to do or say, until it was all over. And in the end we simply embraced in silence, two souls who had lost their way.

Why must all things pass? I lie beside you and I cry, softly, for the love that never again shall be.

$$* * *$$

A pulsar is a rotating neutron star which emits radiation in the form of radio waves, X-rays, or gamma rays. The radiation emitted has a regular period (the pulse).

Using a radio telescope which I built that spring, I scanned the heavens. Each sweep of the night sky took four days and produced four hundred feet of chart paper which I would spend the next week analyzing. I was looking for something unusual. I didn't know what, but I knew I would know it when I came upon it.

I discovered the first pulsar on May 6. The pulse took up one inch of the four-hundred-foot chart. I named the pulsar LGM-1 (Little Green Men 1), in honor of the Martians I had discovered decades before.

For the next several weeks I monitored the pulsar, taking measurements and charting the results. Pulsar LGM-1 rotated once every 3 seconds. Its magnetic field was one trillion times stronger than Earth's. The magnetic field's axis was not aligned with the pulsar's rotational axis. This resulted in the production of an electric field of approximately one trillion volts. The electric field accelerated electrons to such high velocities that radiation pulses occurred at approximately the same rate as the rotation of the pulsar.

The signal was accompanied by a secondary signal that occurred once a second, like pulsations from a lighthouse, signals I believed might be evidence of an extraterrestrial civilization. A cosmic warning post. But what was the warning? It required further investigation!

When I visited LGM-1 I discovered that it was the central star of a solar system that was made up of eighteen planets: twelve gaseous and six terrestrial. And it was on the fifth of the terrestrial planets, a planet twice the size of Earth, that I found evidence of an ancient, advanced, and now quite dead civilization. I discovered wondrous treasures: enormous telescopes the size of cities, museums that displayed exotic plant and animal life, libraries filled with books detailing inventions and scientific theorems mankind could never have dreamed of. I named the dead planet Rhea in honor of the daughter of Uranus and Gaea, the wife and sister of Cronus, and the mother of Zeus, Poseidon, Hera, Hades, Demeter, and Hestia.

* * *

But wherever shall I go, Isabella? Whatever shall I do? Though I travel far and wide, my loss only deepens. Love is a blessing if the object of one's love is close at hand, but a curse if she lives on the other side of the cosmos. Memory is all that remains and there is not a blessed thing one can do but dream. Did you know that the ancient Greeks used the same word to express a concept and its opposite?

* * *

The Cat's Eye Nebula is a mere three thousand light years from Earth. It is the most complex nebula in the universe. The Cat's Eye consists of a brilliant central star—NGC 6543—ten thousand times as luminous as our own sun—that orbits a second, less luminous but more massive, companion. The companion is literally ripping mass from the central star—twenty trillion tons per second—mass which is flung far and wide by an intense stellar wind. The material has formed intricate structures: high-speed gas jets, gas shells, and gas knots. These structures form the nebula itself. The gas is so hot it is hollowing out the center of the Cat's Eye. Surrounding the nebula is a series of concentric rings that extend in all directions. Surrounding the rings is a halo that trails off into nothingness.

I enjoy flying around these vast rings that sweep the heavens in wild and eccentric orbits. Up close I see that the nebula has an onion-like structure; it contains dozens of shells that revolve around the central star. Each shell has its own set of rings, its own set of jets, its own set of knots. All in lovely shades of green and red. Taken as a whole it resembles a galactic kaleidoscope.

Sadly, the Cat's Eye Nebula is dying. The vacated center is rapidly expanding into the outer rings and halo. In another thousand years they too will have been vaporized and all that will remain of this beautiful object will be the cold dead central star. Eventually that too will fade.

Adios, Cat's Eye.

Ciao.

* * *

Love can be a garden overgrown with weeds or a garden weeded with care. True love is always of the latter variety. True love demands attention. True love demands time. Not a little here a little there, but constant nourishment and devotion throughout the years. A greater commitment than most of us are willing to make. This is why true love is so rare in the world today. True love's most precious trait is its persistence: true love endures. Nothing can overcome it, subdue it, shackle it, suppress it. Like the petals of a flower it may be scattered widely by the wind, but when kissed by the lips of God it will gracefully bloom again. True love is not to be confused with infatuation which, though true, does not endure. To reach the dizzying heights of romantic bliss only to be thrown upon the rocks of discord and decay is a fate not to be taken lightly! And yet we spend our lives repeatedly going through such episodes. Like lovesick youths we wander first to the left then to the right, seeking the nourishment of love for our impoverished souls. But in our haste we discover too late we have misrepresented the problem, misstated the goal. It was not love but the fulfillment of our own desires that we were after.

See that woman barefoot and alone under the weeping willow tree. See the tears of molten lead roll softly down her cheeks. Comfort her and you shall find, deep within her languid eyes, the answers you have long been seeking. Love is a joy, not a burden. It is a cross, a message boldly written on the fabric of creation: "Nurture me and ye shall grow, dismiss me and ye shall perish." Love is all we can affect, but it is also all that matters.

And then there is my undying love for you. An act of faith in a faithless world. See how I lay myself down in the forest, open my knapsack and pull out the knife, cut open my veins to bleed for you until I die.

* * *

When I finished, Mrs. Brooks nodded. "She sounds like a remarkable woman," she said. "It's a pity you lost her. I'm glad you've written this down. It must bring solace on these cold, winter nights. . . ."

"Yes," I said. "It does."

My eyes are closed, I do not hear her leave; already my mind is a million light years away.

I must have retired for the night and drifted off to sleep, for when I awoke—it was 2 A.M.—I found myself alone in bed in my home on the outskirts of Peoria. I was drenched in sweat. I jumped up and ran throughout the house, looking for my wife. Isabella was not there. Isabella shall never be there. Isabella has run away with a singularity.

THE DAWN OF TIME

The universe came into existence from nothing fourteen billion years ago.

Existence was a point. A quantum fluctuation in the fabric of space-time.

Just as people once thought the earth was flat—and wondered what was beyond the edge of the world—so people today wonder what was before the beginning of time. And the answer is: nothing!

Imagine the earth. The dawn of time is analogous to the point which corresponds to the South Pole. You ask: what is south of the South Pole? And I answer—truthfully—nothing is south of the South Pole. In the same way, before the beginning of the universe—before the Big Bang—there was nothing.

The moment when the universe came into being, all that existed was concentrated in a point. This was the beginning of time. It was like the South Pole of the earth. As time progressed the universe expanded. It formed a cone that grew larger and larger—just like the latitudes of the earth grow larger the further one travels from the South

Pole. A slice of the cone cut at right angles to the cone itself, at any point in time, was analogous to a moment of existence, with the largest slice being the present moment.

At some point in the future the universe will reach its greatest size and then it will begin to contract. This moment of greatest size of the universe corresponds to the latitude of the equator on Earth.

The universe contracts from this point onward—but time still moves forward. Eventually the universe shrinks to a point—a singularity—the North Pole of our Earth analogy. And then it will wink out. Time will have ended.

Does the cycle repeat? That is something that is unknowable because it would take place in another time and place. But if it is true, it is easy to see that this birth and death of universes mirrors the birth and death of everything else: of galaxies, of nebulae, of interplanetary objects, of interstellar space, of quasars, of planets, of stars, of constellations, of supernovas, of pulsars, and of ourselves.

Look closely at the map of the sky. It is the blueprint for the structure of the universe. We are the product of quantum fluctuations in the very early universe.

We are the pulse of the cosmos.

Thank you for listening to me.

XI

JOURNEY TO ANDROMEDA

I discovered a frightening fact the other day. The Andromeda Galaxy is on a collision course with the Milky Way. Andromeda is more massive than the Milky Way and will obliterate it in three billion years. Everything that has ever been and everything that will ever be will vanish at that time. The plays of William Shakespeare. The cantatas of Johann Sebastian Bach. The statues of Michelangelo. The paintings of Picasso. The scientific articles of Franz Herbert. I put my head in my hands and cried.

For awhile. And then I realized if I did nothing about it, well, nothing ever would be done. I would have to put my study of light beams on hold; I would return to it one day. . . .

And so I climbed into my ship and headed out into the cosmos. My destination: the Andromeda galaxy. My mission: to save the Milky Way!

Andromeda is our nearest galactic neighbor. Even so, it is a good three million light-years distant. It is approaching us at a speed of roughly 300,000 miles per hour. It strikes me how odd this is: when we look at the night sky, we see the Andromeda Galaxy as it was three million years ago. During that three-million-year period it has been speeding towards us. Thus it is considerably closer than it appears. It may be nearly on top of us by now! I shudder; I must proceed with all due speed.

* * *

Chaos created the four pillars of the universe: Eros, Tartarus, Erebus, and Gaia. Eros, Tartarus, and Erebus had no offspring. Gaia, however, gave birth to Uranus. Uranus did not have a father; Gaia produced him spontaneously. Out of pity, Uranus married his mother. They had many children who became the first of the Titans, the original rulers of Heaven and Earth. This was long ago when there were no stars in the sky.

Uranus was the first king of the Titans. But he hated his offspring and cast many of them, including the fifty-headed Hecatoncheires and the one-eyed Cyclopes, into Tartarus, the lowest region of the world, as far beneath Earth as Heaven is above. Others he horridly tormented. One day Gaia could take no more. She gave her son Cronus a sickle with jagged teeth. When she was lying with Uranus, Cronus appeared and castrated his father and cast his body into Tartarus. Cronus became the second king of the Titans. He married his sister Rhea. She gave birth to five children: Hestia, Zeus, Poseidon, Hades, and Demeter.

These were the first of the Olympians.

Cronus did not want to be overthrown by one of his children as had happened to his father. So he ate each of his offspring as they were born. Eventually Rhea could take his behavior no more and when Zeus was born she gave Cronus a rock wrapped in clothes to swallow instead. He promptly shoved it down his throat.

Some time later Cronus vomited up the children he had eaten. They fled with Zeus and Rhea to the island of Crete. When Zeus was eighteen he led a revolt against Cronus and the other Titans. The Titans fought from

Mount Othrys and the Olympians from Mount Olympus. The battle raged for ten years, with neither side gaining a clear advantage. One day Zeus had a masterful idea: he went to Tartarus and freed the Hecatoncheires and the Cyclopes.

Out of gratitude, the Cyclopes gave Zeus thunder and lightning; they gave Hades a helmet and Poseidon a trident. The Hecatoncheires gave the other Olympian gods missiles. With these weapons the Olympians were able to overthrow the Titans. They banished the Titans to Tartarus where the Hecatoncheires watch over them to this day.

* * *

I have seen many beautiful sights in the universe, but nothing matches the beauty of the Andromeda Galaxy. My jaw drops in astonishment as I approach this galactic wonder. It is a classic spiral galaxy, like our own Milky Way, 250,000 light-years in diameter. I see intricate spiral arms, an off-center ring of star formation, globular and open clusters, interstellar debris, planetary nebulae, and supernova remnants.

From Earth, Andromeda is visible to the naked eye; it is the most distant astronomical object detectable in such a manner. Yet it appears quite small. Now I see how much larger it actually is: only the central part is bright enough to be seen from Earth; the rest of the galaxy is hidden from view by enormous clouds of interstellar dust. I pass through the dust and see the galaxy in all its splendor.

M31, as it is technically known, has an interesting history. It was known to the Persian astronomer Abd-al-Rahman Al-Sufi about 905 AD. He described it as a "small cloud." It appeared on Johann Stevan's Star Map in 1500 but he gave it no name. It was described by Simon Marius in 1612, by Giovanni Batista Hodierna in 1654, and by

Ishmael Bouilland in 1661. These "discoverers" wrongly thought Andromeda was not a galactic neighbor, but rather a nebula in our own Milky Way. It wasn't until 1923 when Edward Hubble established the intergalactic distance between it and the Milky Way, using Cepheid variable stars. He was off by a factor of two (he thought it only 1.5 million light-years distant), but I won't fault him for that—the instruments at his disposal were primitive.

* * *

After the Titans had been overthrown Zeus became ruler of the Gods. It happened this way: Zeus and his brothers drew lots to decide how the universe would be divided up. Poseidon drew the sea; Hades the underworld; Zeus the heavens. Since Zeus had rescued his brothers and sisters, they made him the protector and ruler of both the gods and the human race.

* * *

I gasp in disbelief at what appears before my eyes. It is a *hole*. A galactic hole in one of the spiral arms of the Andromeda Galaxy.

I neglected to tell you, Isabella, that there is another galaxy, a compact dwarf, in orbit around Andromeda. M32, "the little one." From Earth, M32 is a small, bluish-green elliptical galaxy that is only about eight thousand light-years in diameter. It is composed almost entirely of very old stars, no dust or debris of any kind. It appears to be a calm and gentle neighbor. But that was then and this is now. I see that in three million light-years it will have smashed through Andromeda, destroying one of the main spiral arms, obliterating old stars and causing new ones to form.

As I approach the hole I feel the shock waves from this collision. The jolts to my ship grow steadily stronger and I become alarmed. I had always thought of Andromeda as a peaceful haven where I could find solace. Ha! Here I was in my spaceship plunging into a galactic black hole—that was what resulted from the collision of M31 and M32. M32 and M31. The M's.

* * *

Zeus is thought to have been all-powerful and wise, but he was neither. He could be, and often was, opposed and tricked by both gods and men. No one was better at manipulating Zeus than Aphrodite, the Goddess of Love. She caused him to fall in love with many women; his numerous affairs only incensed his wife, Hera, and caused him no end of grief.

Hera was very beautiful. She was, in fact, one of the three contestants in the Judgment of Paris which led to the Trojan War. But Zeus married her through trickery and for that she never forgave him. Here is how it happened: Zeus had courted Hera for years, but she would have nothing to do with him. One day he turned himself into an injured bird. When Hera came upon the bird she felt sorry for it and held it to her breast. Zeus seized the moment, turned himself back into a god, and had his way with her. Out of shame she agreed to marry him. It was a marriage doomed from the beginning.

Hera was always complaining and harassing Zeus who eventually grew weary of her company and began to stray. When Hera realized what was happening she convinced the other gods to revolt against him. She drugged her husband and, while he was sleeping, tied him to a couch. Then she called the other gods and left her husband to his fate. They could not decide who would take Zeus' place and began to quarrel. A young god named Briareus, who was still loyal to his ruler, took the opportunity to untie the knots. Zeus sprang up and threatened the other gods with his thunderbolt. When they told him Hera had plotted against him, he seized her and hung her from Orion's Belt with gold chains. He said he would destroy anyone who tried to free her. Of course, no one dared. Eventually Zeus grew tired of her weeping, and, after she agreed never to conspire against him, he set her free.

Zeus had so many lovers that a reliable count will never be known. But his divine wives are known:

His first wife was Metis. She bore him a daughter named Athena. Zeus promptly ate his daughter for it had been prophesied she would bear a son who would overthrow her father.

His second wife was Themis. She gave birth to Dice, Eirene, Eunomia, Morae, Clotho, and Lachesis.

Third came Eurynome. She bore three daughters known as the Graces: Aglaia, Euphrosyne, and Thalia.

Next came Mnemosyne who gave birth to nine daughters, the Muses.

Zeus' fifth wife was his daughter Demeter with whom he fathered Persephone.

The sixth wife was Leto. She gave Zeus twins, Apollo and Artemis.

Hermes was born to Maia, his seventh wife, she the daughter of Atlas.

And finally there was Hera, the eighth and final wife. She gave Zeus two sons, Ares and Hephaestus, and two daughters, Hebe and Eileithyia.

At this point Zeus grew weary of goddesses and began falling in love with mortal women. He often appeared disguised as a bull or other mammal and took his conquest by surprise. Hera knew of his affairs but was unable to stop him and unwilling to leave. Two of the more famous earthly offspring were Hercules, by Alcmene, and Dionysus, by Sememe.

* * *

I have written extensively about the Greek gods and now I will tell you why. It has to do with the space-time continuum. I have come to realize that the gods and goddesses were entities from another universe who one day gained the ability to enter our universe. I said earlier that couldn't be done, and man certainly cannot do so, but if beings live long enough they become gods and can do anything. The gods transported themselves to our world and became its protectors and benefactors. They were worshipped as gods because they were gods.

In a sense they were like me, living in two places at once. How I would have liked to talk with them. I've often wondered if I'm one of their descendants. Is it possible my seizures are due to this? I recall that list of famous epileptics throughout history which the doctor recited along with my initial diagnosis: Julius Caesar, Vincent van Gogh, Theodore Dostoyevsky, Peter the Great, Charles Dickens, Isaac Newton, Sir Walter Scott, and Jonathan Swift. What did they have in common? They lived in two worlds! Did they—like me—feel torn apart? It is fascinating to think about, but it will never be known because they are no more.

* * *

I feared this would happen. While I am ruminating on the loves of Zeus I stray too close to Andromeda's center and an enormous black hole. I am being drawn into the hole and there is nothing I can do to stop it. I realize that by the time Andromeda reaches the Milky Way—in three billion years—it will have become a galactic vacuum cleaner—a second Pluto Redux—only this time it will be several times larger than the Milky Way. It will consume a helpless Earth. I smile at my vindication (I had been right after all—only three billion years too soon!).

The black hole is emitting X-rays at a prodigious rate. It is extremely hot as well. My instruments measure its thermal temperature at millions of degrees Kelvin. I watch in fascination as a star slowly orbits the event horizon. It circles round and round, nearer and nearer, like a coin in a funnel. And then—in the wink of an eye—it is gone. Nothing to indicate it ever was. There is, however, a blip on my X-ray device when the star is digested by the hole. I shudder. Is this to be my fate?

Apparently, I am about to find out, for without warning my ship lurches forward as if caught in a gravitational beam; a cry escapes my lips—"Isabella! I have always loved you!"—and my ship is sucked into the black hole with a swoosh and a roar and everything winks out. Everything. Out.

IT'S NOT WHAT YOU THINK IT IS (A MEDITATION ON TIME)

(January 28, 1968)

I hold my hand before me. In five seconds, I can move it to the left or the right or I can leave it where it is. It is my choice.

One. Two. Three. Four. Five.

I move it to the right.

It was my choice.

Or was it?

I repeat the experiment and this time move it to the left demonstrating that I possess free will—when I realize my error. The second experiment occurred at a different point in time. To show that I possess free will I would have to go back in time and repeat the experiment. But that is impossible for time moves inexorably forward; in other words, I cannot go back in time and repeat the experiment simply because I cannot go back in time. It does not follow, however, that if I could go back in time and repeat the experiment I could pick a different outcome. The solution is not knowable.

So perhaps I do not possess free will after all. But if I do not possess free will, if everything is preordained, then my life is merely an unwinding. The tick-tock of a great cosmic clock. That would be a very sad state of affairs, which leads me to my meditation.

* * *

"It's not what you think it is," Chancy said as he tossed a red rubber ball into the air. I admired the gentle arc the ball made as it rose and then fell back into his hirsute hand. He repeated the maneuver.

Before I could tell him what I thought it might be, he continued, "It's not a rubber ball, you know, it's a spaceship and it's on its way to Neptune." And with a wail like a banshee he hurled the ball into a cloudless sky.

And I saw that it really *was* a spaceship. I admired the yellow flame of the rocket's engine, the white exhaust plume that trailed across the sky's deep-blue dome.

"When will it reach that dark forbidden planet?" I asked. "And what will it do when it gets there?"

"A trip to Neptune takes about a dozen years," my friend replied. "Unfortunately, this particular ship will never make it. My toss was off. Jupiter's gravity will alter the rocket's trajectory and fling it out of the solar system." He sighed. "Let's try another." He pulled a second ball from his pocket and with a marking pen wrote today's date in bold black numbers across the surface of the ball. Then he hurled it into the sky. "Much better," he said as it disappeared from view.

Chancy looked at me and smiled. "But bother all that —would *you* like to go?" He turned to one side and I was surprised to see a rocket ship, perhaps fifty feet tall, its surface sleek and shiny. The main tank was painted purple, red, and gold, and the oval capsule gleamed in pretty shades of violet. How could I not have noticed it before?"

* * *

"You never answered my second question," I said to Chancy as we moved past the orbit of Uranus, the sideways planet. "What are we to *do* on Neptune?"

"Neptune has no solid surface, as I'm sure you know," my friend replied. "It's nothing but a vast blue ocean. At least that's what astronomers have always believed. But this is not the first mission to the planet. Unmanned ships detected islands in the ocean. Most quickly come and go, Neptune's turbulent tides overwhelming them, but there's one island, which I've dubbed Ajax, which is much larger than the others and has remained since it was first detected two years ago."

I felt the thrill of adventure swell within me. "How glorious!" I cried.

"And that's not all. There's an entity on the island, a being of some sort. We have corresponded for several months. His name is Erasmus and his title is Ruler of the Oceans of Neptune. He is eager to meet us."

I didn't know what I expected—I hoped it would be something sublime—but when we landed three days later, I was surprised to discover that Erasmus was not an exotic alien, nor an almighty god, nor a sage wizard, but an ordinary man. A very old man. A very old man with majestic silver-and-gold wings that glistened in the pale light of day. (They were needed, I surmised, to fly from one island to the next.)

"We made it," Chancy said, triumphantly, as Erasmus bowed before us in greeting.

The old man was holding a silver trident in his left hand. His gray beard was well-groomed. He had large light-green eyes. Sad eyes. Eyes that seemed to reflect the very depths of the ocean over which he ruled. He looked familiar, though I did not see how this could be. Something about the shape of his face, the prognathous jaw, the sloping forehead, the sunken cheeks, or was it those eyes, eyes which were so full of meaning?

Ah—but it was what he held in his right hand that amazed—no, *frightened*—me: one of Chancy's red balls. Pitted in spots—no doubt from the voyage—but undoubtedly his. The large black numerals indicating the launch date were clearly visible.

"I believe this is yours," Erasmus said, in perfect English, as he held out the ball to my friend. "It arrived only yesterday. Your calculations were most exact. I congratulate you."

"Yes," Chancy said as he took the proffered object. He checked the date and harrumphed. "The ball I sent your way the day before we left."

"How can that possibly be?" I asked, incredulously. "You said it would be a voyage of a dozen years. Ours took only a week and yet the ball arrived *before* us."

Chancy let loose a boisterous laugh and his blue eyes twinkled. He looked over at Erasmus, who seemed lost in thought. "That's because you think of time in a literal sense," Chancy said. "Whereas it is really elastic. It can stretch or contract and be none the wiser."

Erasmus laid down his trident and opened his arms as if in explication. "In a very real sense, there's no such thing as Time. You know this intuitively—sometimes the days pass fast, sometimes slow—though intellectually it is a concept few can grasp. We seem ruled by time, though we are not."

Chancy picked up the thread. "The ball is the key, as you surmised. And though it arrived before our ship, it traveled through a different dimensional space, one in which the distance from A to B is one-twelfth the distance of the space through which we passed. There was no contradiction."

"Quite so," Erasmus interjected. "And when Chancy asked you what the ball was, it wasn't a rhetorical question. It was both a ball *and* a ship. And a trillion other things."

I wasn't quite sure what he was getting at but Chancy seemed to understand, for he nodded. The bond of complicity between them was all too apparent.

At that moment there was a loud noise, like a clap of thunder only more intense than any I'd heard on Earth. I nearly jumped out of my skin.

"Don't be alarmed," Erasmus said. "It merely heralds the arrival of what must be."

As if on cue, the azure skies opened and I beheld a sight such as no human has ever witnessed: a beam of light, a vast Neptunian rainbow, stretching from east to west. And astride the beam I saw—or thought I saw—a rocket ship much like the ship that brought us here. It was much larger, though, perhaps a mile in length. It gleamed a brilliant silver in the soft light of the beam.

And as I watched in fascination, I saw that the ship was moving slowly across the sky, only it was not the ship that was moving, it was the beam of light carrying the ship in its wake.

Several minutes passed and then the beam began to fade, dissipating into a shimmering mist of color and light.

And through it all, Chancy and Erasmus gazed absentmindedly at the great blue-gray ocean of Neptune, oblivious, apparently, to the spectacle unfolding above us. And though they themselves were separated by a vast gulf of time, they seemed somehow entangled by time, like cosmic particles that are simultaneously here and there—now and then—and thus everywhere and always. And it was then that I began to appreciate what they had been telling me. It was only for a moment—a tantalizing insight, quickly forgotten—and I was once again conscious of the ocean's waves. I found myself alone on the shore of an island in the great Neptunian Ocean.

Yes, both of my hosts had vanished! One would have expected me to have been terrified—thirty billion miles from Earth with no hope of returning—but it really wasn't that way. There was something peaceful about this planet, and its never-ending ocean, and, after a period of sober reflection, I lay down on the sand and simply gazed at the water's great expanse.

It was sometime later when I saw Chancy and Erasmus, loping towards me along the shore. They were deep in conversation—both were gesticulating animatedly—perhaps a dialogue on the nature of time? And suddenly I realized why Erasmus had looked familiar: he was an image of my friend many years in the future. Whether he existed or not was anyone's guess. The implications were troubling, though, and I forced them from my mind.

It might have been because of the soothing Neptunian waves, or the long day I'd had, or both, but at that moment my eyelids grew heavy and soon I was fast asleep, dreaming of the fiery stars and the endless universe.

When I opened my eyes, I found myself back on Earth in one of the many cornfields that rimmed Peoria. I was surprised and delighted at my good fortune. I saw no sign of Chancy (Erasmus, I knew, would never leave his home), but I did see something else. Before me, nestled amongst the swaying stalks, I spied a wooden trident and a red rubber ball. And I knew at once what I had to do. I picked up the trident and broke it in two. Then I cast the rubber ball into a silvery sky. That was several years ago and I am still awaiting its return.

* * *

You see, Isabella, time is like a river that winds its way to the sea and the grains of sand that line the shore are but another reminder of the divisibility of the cosmos.

XII

THE DISPLACED MAN

Three things puzzle me after I cross into the black hole. I had expected it to be pitch-dark, but it is not. The space around me is as bright as before I entered. If it was not for the distortion that is everywhere I would not know I had gone from there (outside the hole) to here (inside the hole).

It occurs to me that I had not been torn apart when I crossed the event horizon and this puzzles me as well.

The third thing that puzzles me is that everything looks blue. On reflection I realize what is happening: as light falls into the black hole it gains energy which results in its wavelength growing shorter. Just inside the event horizon light has infinite energy and zero wavelength. Everything is as blue as blue can be!

Looking back towards the horizon I see the universe unfold before my eyes. There is Earth. There is Harvard University. There is Watertown. There is Isabella. She watched as I drew near the black hole (though, of course, she will never see me enter—the light from my fall will take an infinite amount of time to reach her). "Hello, Isabella!" I cry. "I am here! I made it!"

The question arises: How do I get out?

Unfortunately, the escape velocity from a black hole is equal to the speed of light—which I can never attain. Perhaps the laws of physics do not apply here. The laws of physics as I understand them. For a moment I am hopeful. My task is to figure out how to accelerate to the speed of light and travel back towards the event horizon. Then I realize I have misstated the problem. It doesn't matter how fast I travel. In a black hole space is curved on itself like a doughnut. No matter how fast I travel I will simply go round in circles. I will be like a penny in a funnel following a circumscribed path that descends towards the singularity that lies at the bottom.

Escape is impossible.

* * *

Galileo Galilei was born on February 15, 1564 in Pisa, Italy. He is known as the father of observational astronomy, and with good reason. He popularized Copernicus' theory that the earth revolved around the Sun and this got him into trouble with the Roman Catholic Church. He improved the telescope and observed the moons of Jupiter in 1610. He developed the theories of motion and acceleration. He was one of the first to observe sunspots. He was the first to observe Neptune, though he didn't realize it was a planet. He reported on lunar mountains and even estimated their height. He deduced that the Milky Way was composed of stars and was not a cloud, the prevailing belief at the time.

Galileo was a devout Catholic but he had three illegitimate children, two of whom he hid away in the convent of San Matteo. Maria Celeste was born on August 16, 1600. A sister, Livia, followed in 1601. Both entered the convent at the age of ten and spent the remainder of their lives there. Maria Celeste was a constant source of support for Galileo and even helped prepare his manuscripts. There is a crater on Venus which is named after her. The third child, a son named Vincenzio, was born in 1606. He was eventually legitimized and married Sestilia Bocchineri.

* * *

An amazing thing has happened: I have stopped moving. I am at a loss to explain why. It is as if I am frozen in space. A very eerie feeling.

My colleagues at Harvard claimed the universe is infinite and expanding, but that never made sense to me. Lost and alone in the infinite expanse of the black hole, I realize why I was troubled. Yes, the universe is infinite. And, yes, space is expanding. But it is not true that the matter in it is moving farther apart at ever increasing speeds (as my Harvard colleagues concluded). Rather, the matter of the universe simply sits there, not moving at all. It is space itself which is stretching, giving the illusion of movement.

But if space itself is stretching, the relative distance between any two points in the universe never changes. And that results in a paradox of cosmic proportions, for it implies that the universe is essentially unchanging as well. It has puffed itself up, but nothing more.

I sit unmoving in the black hole and I think of things like this. You may think I'm mad, Isabella, but given my current plight, what else am I to do?

There is a sudden jolt and once again I am moving forward. Apparently, the singularity has noticed my presence and is drawing me in. As I approach, I formulate a theory. It had been mulling about in my brain for some time, but now that I'm here—in the black hole—I wonder if perhaps it's true: *is the singularity a gateway to another dimensional space?*

If only I could communicate my theory to Earth! If true, it would herald a scientific revolution unlike any other. But communication from a black hole is impossible. I am trapped here. Or rather, the only place I can go is through that gateway and into another time and place.

It is a tremendous opportunity—one that surely will not come my way again—and so I will take it. When I arrive at the gateway, I will step lightly through, knowing not what lies beyond.

* * *

Galileo maintained that the Sun was the center of the universe, not the earth. The church considered this heresy and ordered him to restate his views. He refused, whereupon the church informed him that he would be subjected to three inquisitions.

Galileo's first inquisition occurred on April 12, 1633. It took place before three judges and lasted five minutes. Galileo was asked whether he knew why he had been cited and he answered in the affirmative. He was then carted off to jail. He was allowed to write to Maria Celeste and she was greatly agitated at the news of his incarceration. Unfortunately, just at this time the plague struck Florence and the authorities instituted a strict quarantine; Maria was not allowed to visit her father.

The second examination took place on April 30. Here Galileo confessed to ignorance of the truth but maintained that he had not been willingly disobedient. He was returned to prison.

The third interrogation occurred on May 10. Galileo was asked the same questions as before and he gave the same answers. The Inquisitors seemed favorably disposed to Galileo. He believed things had finally turned in his favor and that he would soon be released. The Pope, however, was convinced Galileo not only believed his past teachings but had every intention of continuing to promote them if he were to be found not guilty. On June 16 the Pope issued a decree ordering a *fourth* examination and said that Galileo would be subjected to torture if he did not unequivocally recant his views.

On June 22, the fourth examination occurred. Galileo was once again read the charges of heresy against him. He was then forced to repeat—word for word—an "admission of guilt" as dictated by the papal office. This he did. But as he was turning to go he muttered the words: "But the earth does move, though."

* * *

Ok, I'll take the bait. What lies beyond the singularity I am fast approaching? If it represents a point at the end of the universe, what then? Is it a place into which I can stick my hand? Or is it literally nothingness?

According to Aristotle the universe is finite and there is nothing outside the cosmos. But I do not agree. If I were to travel to the end of the cosmos and stand on my spacecraft and extend my hand, is Aristotle saying my hand would no longer exist because it was being thrust into—nothingness? It is more likely that by extending my hand into the beyond I *create* the space into which it is thrust.

This state of affairs exists not only at the *edge* but *throughout* the universe, that is, we create space as we move through time. How we perceive the universe is an adaptation we make to keep from going mad. In this scenario, the universe is not continuous—as we perceive it—rather, it is a series of discontinuities (I recall those ancient paradoxes of continuity and discontinuity). What lies beyond the edge of the universe is no different from what lies inside the universe. And thus—in a sense—Aristotle was correct after all.

I do not know what lies beyond the universe, but I can imagine it. And I imagine it not as eternal blackness, but as eternal whiteness, an empty canvas where nothing exists. But, then again, perhaps it is neither, perhaps it is something else, something I cannot fathom.

* * *

Sentencing was swift: Galileo was found guilty of all charges. His works were banned as were any future works he might write. He was ordered to recite the seven Penitential Psalms once a week for the remainder of his days. Then he was imprisoned in a castle tower in Siena. The sentence was read publicly in Inquisition Hall and at universities throughout Italy, thus publicly humiliating not only Galileo but also all those who had shared his beliefs.

"My name is erased from the book of the living," Galileo lamented in a letter to Maria Celeste.

"Do not speak thus for it is not so," she replied. "If for a brief moment your name and fame are clouded, believe that they will one day be restored to greater brightness."

* * *

I have divided the life of the universe into four eras. The first is the Formative Era. Here space comes into being and expands rapidly. Quarks and electrons form, then protons and neutrons. These particles clump together to form atoms, the building blocks of matter.

We live in the second era, the Star-Filled era. It is filled with all I have herein described: stars, nebulae, interplanetary objects, galaxies, quasars, constellations, supernovas,

222

asteroids, pulsars, planets, and interstellar space. It contains Life. Civilization. Poetry. Music.

The third era I have termed the Degenerate Era. In this era everything is falling apart. The universe is filled with dead and dying things: cold planets, white dwarfs, neutron stars, interstellar debris. Matter is decomposing. Life still exists but it is formless, thoughtless.

The fourth and final era is the Black Hole Era. The only remaining objects are black holes. They slowly evaporate and eventually disappear. Nothing remains. No one will be around to witness the death of the universe for the simple fact that nothing exists to put anyone together to witness it.

* * *

It was on the 3d of December that the Pope decided to move Galileo from the city of Siena—where he was still well-known and revered—to Arcetri, a villa in the countryside near Florence, where his influence would be less. This was also near San Matteo, the convent where his two daughters had been placed. Galileo was allowed frequent visits, but alas, tragedy struck here as well: Maria Celeste had been so attentive to the illness that was all around her that she paid little attention to her own health and was finally overcome by dysentery, dying after six days on April 1, 1634.

In his new prison, Galileo was as despondent as ever. He wrote to Cardinal Barberino on July 13:

"I detest the remembrance of the time I have consumed in study. I regret ever having published what I wrote, and all that I have yet by me."

Sadly it appears Galileo did indeed carry out his wishes, at least in part, for none of his later communications with Cardinal Barberino—which were said to include descriptions of several major new discoveries—have ever been found.

Galileo died on January 8, 1642 at the age of seventy-seven of natural causes, exactly one hundred years after the death of Copernicus.

I have always felt an affinity for Galileo. He was right about what he believed and the forces allied against him were wrong.

* * *

Light stretches as it travels through the universe, its wavelength increasing. Therefore, it grows more red. We measure the wavelength of light when it was emitted and when it was received and we subtract the two to determine the degree of this reddening. This change in wavelength tells us how much the universe has stretched between the time light was emitted to the time it was received. Say, for example, that I am on a beam of light that leaves Galaxy A and arrives at Galaxy B one hundred light-years later. Say, also, that the space through which the light traveled expanded to four times its original size. I would have traveled not one hundred light-years, but four hundred. This red shift, as it is called, is defined to be one less than the factor by which the universe has expanded. In this example, the red shift is three.

Any galaxy moving faster than a red shift of 1.4 (which really isn't that much) is moving faster than light. Since nothing can move faster than light, how can that be? It's obvious if you think about it; it is due to the universe's expansion. It's impossible to move through space faster than the speed of light on small scales (planets or stars). But at huge distances the effect of the universe's expansion becomes significant. *Space itself* is expanding to such a degree that the relative distances between galaxies are increasing faster than the speed of light—as measured by a red shift of greater than 1.4. Note that this has no effect on the galaxies themselves (that is, on the planets and stars that make up the galaxies) since they aren't really moving anyway. There is a point at which the light from these receding galaxies will never reach us. In effect, they disappear from the universe. This point is the universe's event horizon.

It is at this moment that all becomes clear to me: the universe is an enormous black hole, a black hole that contains other black holes—one of which I am in right now. I have hypothesized about whether black holes are gateways to other places. I may be wrong, I may be right. But at this point it doesn't matter. I am about to enter the singularity of this black hole. I am about to find out what, if anything, lies beyond.

CREATION

(May 30, 1971)

To paraphrase Albert Einstein, "The gods and goddesses do not play dice with the universe." This may be true but it is also misleading, for the gods and the goddesses *are* the universe. That is, the sum total of all that there is *is* the universe, *are* the celestial deities. And we, being part of the universe, are therefore part of this part.

I am a collection of atomic particles, whirling about. Atomic particles are mainly empty space with bits of stuff here and there. But mostly nothingness. This is me. Other particles pass through me all the time and I don't even notice. In fact, it is not clear what is the I that is me.

I am a collection of particles. And yet the whole that is me—that is Franz Herbert—is merely a single particle in the whole that is the universe.

The electrons whirl around the atom as the planets orbit their sun as their sun orbits the black hole that lies at the center of their galaxy as the galaxy orbits its local group of galaxies as the local group orbits the center of Creation. And what is Creation but the beginning of *that* which gave birth to *this* out of which *I* arose?

I don't know my place in the universe but I do know that I am here, that I occupy space and time, that I love Isabella, and that one day the I that is me shall be no more.

There is another possibility though, and one which I cannot discount: that I *myself* am a god and am eternal. But I cannot accept this. It would imply not only that I am now but also that I always have been. And I know this is not the case. It is enough to know that I occupy space and time for a brief instant.

Another possibility (among the infinite possibilities that might explain Creation) is that the universe, which we think of as a limitless expanse, is not limitless, but is instead like a drop of water in a meta-cosmic ocean, or, an even better analogy, like a mud puddle on the surface of an existence that is itself unknowable.

One could go on like this forever and yet never be closer to the truth. I am a flame, a flame that flickered brightly for a while and now is slowly dying.

You ask how it feels to be me, to be Franz Herbert, and I reply (truthfully, though you seem to feel I am making light of the question) that I don't know how it feels *not* to be me. I am not some insect that crawls through your garden taking up space and time. Or maybe I am. Maybe that is all that I am. Maybe there is no difference between me and a blister beetle.

XIII

THE LAST PHOTON

I emerge from the black hole into the blackness of space. It is an immense, all-encompassing darkness and I shudder. I have experienced darkness such as this only once before, when I was in Mammoth Cave in southwestern Illinois. Our guide thought it would be amusing to turn off the lights that lit up the cavern. For a full minute we were in total darkness. Not a single photon to see by. A year of this and one would go blind, the guide said, and laughed.

And then he took me aside and whispered into my ear: Pluto is not a planet because it does not reside in the zodiac.

This may be so, I tell him; however, it has been in the zodiac my entire life, in the constellation Ophiuchus, a constellation people say is not a zodiacal constellation because Ptolemy did not include it in his list. But that is hardly a scientific explanation.

Hmm, he continued, what do we have here? A planet that is not a planet, a constellation that is not a constellation, *an astronomer who is not an astronomer.*

This is what I've had to contend with my entire life.

* * *

Thanatos was the god of Death, though he is rarely spoken of in myth. He is not to be confused with Hades who was the god of the underworld. Rather, Thanatos was the personification of death. He was the son of Nyx and the twin brother of Hypnos. He was hideous, painful, cruel, brooding, mocking, and malignant.

Thanatos was the most hated of the gods because he took away life. If one were lucky he came in old age, though he could come at any time, and he often did so without warning. The only thing known for certain is that he would come one day.

* * *

My spaceship has vanished—it was eaten up by the black hole—and I have been left to fend for myself. I am perched atop a beam of light, hurtling through the vacuum of space. It is odd, but I am not afraid. I feel safe atop this beam, charging ahead at a speed of 186,000 miles per second. I shall think no more of my life on Earth, of my wife and child whom I have left behind.

A beam of light is an interesting phenomenon. This one is two feet wide and six feet thick. Rays emanate from all sides, top and bottom. The amount of energy in a beam of light is dependent on the source of the light. With the beacon that is the Sun, the energy is about 15,000 watts per square foot. This beam is much cooler than that. There is a feeling of gentle warmth coursing through. I have no idea where this beam originated, but I note that it contains all the colors of the rainbow. Perhaps it was shot from the black hole itself and contains everything that ever was.

Richard of York Gave Battle in Vain. That is how we remember the colors of the rainbow: Red, Orange, Yellow,

Green, Blue, Indigo, and Violet. I have never ridden a prettier beam of light. I am a cosmic traveler and I am in a real mess now. I would fall on my knees and pray except that I am already on my knees and all the gods I would pray to are dead.

* * *

I know what you're thinking: you're thinking I'm crazy and what I need is a good therapist. The truth of the matter is this: what I am experiencing is the final stage of a disease which has slowly been devouring me. I hear voices. I see the face of Isabella as she looks down on me, and that of Jason, too. Who are they but two Charons to guide me across the river to Hades which lies on the other shore?

I reach out to touch a face but there is no one there.

I call out the name of Isabella but she does not answer.

Neither does my son respond to my cries.

Are they there? Do they hear me?

Do they hear and ignore me?

As everyone ignores me.

Me, the forgotten, the cast-aside.

I recall the last time I saw Isabella. It was the day after she said she was leaving me. You might think I would be upset, but I wasn't at all. I felt relieved. Instead of trying to be something I was not—a husband—this would free me to be what I truly was: a cosmic traveler. At the same time I was saddened for I loved Isabella more than anything in the cosmos.

* * *

As I hurtle through the cosmos on a beam of light, I feel myself fading and I realize what is happening. I can see through myself now, through my flesh. It is rather unsettling. I must write rapidly before my fingers fade and there will be no more words. The beam begins to dissipate and it is not long before I am upon the last of the last. The last ray of light. The last photon. I had always thought that when death was imminent I would recall the main events of my life, but this does not happen. I am fascinated only by what lies before me. A never-ending darkness, a coldness, a void. "Hi-ho!" I cry as I rush headlong into that space from which I will never return.

Everything around me dissipates and it is as it was before the very beginning.

* * *

It is not known how Zeus died. It is not even known if Zeus died, for it has always been believed that the gods are immortal. Even so that does not mean they will always rule over Earth and over Heaven and Hell.

I, however, have come to believe that Zeus is no more —that he does not exist as you and I know existence—and I try to imagine his death. Perhaps he grew tired of Hera's haranguing. She was a jealous woman and he was never really free to do as he wished.

Perhaps he grew weary of mediating between gods and men. The conflicts between them were constant and I can only imagine the energy he expended to keep the peace.

Perhaps his brothers, Poseidon and Hades, envious of his supreme position, waged war against him, overthrew him after a war that lasted many years, and exiled him from Olympus.

Or perhaps it was more mundane. Perhaps he simply grew old and left of his own accord. Shuffled off the godly stage.

Of course all this begs the question: where *do* gods go when they die? They cannot retire to Tartarus or the Elysian Fields, for they rule over those lands—they would never really have left! The gods, one would imagine, have their own resting place. A place where they can frolic forever.

But I do not believe that this is so. I think even gods tire of being gods. They yearn for another place. A place where they are alone, isolated from the world of man and from each other.

There are places not known to men and it is there that the gods retire, places so foreign to the human mind that they cannot even be imagined. I think I am entering such a place now.

$$* * *$$

The last lucid thoughts of a dying man, the last imaginings of one who soon will be no more. . . . The universe is in oscillation. From the explosion that created the matter which coalesced into our world came the space that we inhabit. This space has been expanding for fourteen billion years but it will not expand forever. Already the expansion is slowing and soon it will come to a dead halt. Then, under the influence of gravity, it will contract until a final implosion takes place fourteen billion years hence. The universe will transform itself into a black hole that collapses into a single point, a singularity. A mathematical construct.

But this is only the beginning. The process repeats. This never-ending sequence of events can be compared to the beating of a human heart which expands and contracts, seemingly forever. Imagine that! Within our own bodies is mirrored the universe in which we live. Will events repeat themselves in subsequent expansions so that billions of years from now I will again find myself on a beam of light that is streaking through the heavens as I pen these very words?

There is more, but I am tired. I must return once more to the world which bore me to pay final homage to Isabella. And I now know what I will tell her: when life is over, it will be like a puff of smoke.

Paff!

The.

End.

THE NIGHT THE ALIENS CAME

(August 30, 1971)

The night the aliens came I was sitting on my front porch, looking out over the cornfields. I saw the constellation Orion low in the eastern sky and a fuzzy patch near the middle star in the sword: the Orion Nebula, a stellar nursery. And from the tip of the sword came a blinding flash, a shooting star that streaked across the sky. It seemed so inconsequential; it had happened many times before. How could I have known it was the place from where the aliens came?

The next morning I came across the aliens' spaceship, a bright silver cylindrical craft, but with no distinguishing markings. The aliens had emerged and were looking out over the cornfields. They did not notice me. (Perhaps they considered me too unimportant to notice?) After a while they got into their craft which rose silently into the air.

I returned to the cornfields night after night and, night after night, the aliens came. One windy evening, when the aliens had wandered off, I drummed up the courage to stow away aboard their vessel. The next morning, we rose up. And up and up and up. A pale dot in a clear blue sky.

As luck would have it, there was a porthole in my hiding place, and I was able to observe the heavens as we passed by. We passed the outer planets of the solar system: the great gas planet Jupiter; Saturn, the home of sorcerers; Uranus, which lay laughing upon its back; and Neptune, that pale blue watery world. For a moment I thought Pluto might be our final destination! Was I lucky enough to have been spirited away by a civilization from the Underworld?

But, alas, we zoomed by.

It seemed that the ship's rate of acceleration only increased. Soon we left the confines of our galaxy, and I found myself in the vastness of space. I felt an emptiness I had experienced many times before. Only this time I spied not a single atom. Was this the place from where the aliens came?

And then what I was afraid was about to happen happened: My mind was here and it was not here. My thoughts were here and they were not here. I found myself in a world that flashed in and out of existence, for consciousness itself had begun to fade.

When I awoke I was back on my front porch, looking out over the cornfields. I felt as if I was one-hundred years old. I thought of Isabella and of how it was before she slipped away. Later that night as I drifted off to sleep, I remembered how it was when I held her close, clinging to her for dear life, the edge of existence fading. Until one day when all would be as if it never really was. Like that misty unforgiving space out of which the aliens came.

POSTSCRIPT

BEING AN ACCOUNT OF THE LIFE OF FRANZ HERBERT AS RECORDED BY DR. JOSEPH ARNOLD, DR. OF PSYCHIATRY, ST. FRANCIS MEDICAL CENTER, PEORIA, ILLINOIS

Professor Pasqual:
Dr. Herbert came to see me in the spring of 1951. He was a patient for nearly two decades. He was forty-five years old when he first appeared, a thin man with a hollow face. His left hand trembled as he spoke and his voice was soft as if it was an echo from another time or place. It took half-a-dozen visits before he opened up about his past: the loss of his wife, the estrangement of his son, his failed career. His self-esteem was low and his outlook on life dim, but I did not consider him suicidal. I suggested weekly sessions, but he came less often. He was frequently elsewhere, he said. It wasn't until later when I learned what he meant.

Herbert's cosmic travels were an enigma as was his odd interest in ancient deities and the degree to which the two intermingled in his mind. By all accounts he was a brilliant man and I was puzzled by his inability—or unwillingness—to focus on the real world. On further reflection perhaps it isn't puzzling at all. Herbert was clearly unable to separate fact from fiction. That his fate should be to vanish from society without explanation should not surprise us.

THE ASTRONOMER

The account which follows may deviate from the true history of events in minor ways—details which I feel compelled to alter or omit —but is, I believe, substantially correct.

Dr. Joseph Arnold

* * *

It was in the constellation Corvus—on a cold, clear winter night—that he found what he had been searching for. "It is done," he sighed. He felt as if an onerous weight had been lifted from his shoulders.

He was sixty-five years old. He spent his days sequestered in his observatory, searching the heavens with a sixteen-inch reflecting telescope, an instrument he had built ten years before.

His name was Franz Herbert. A name known throughout the astronomical world. At the age of twenty-four he had discovered the outermost planet of our solar system, which he dubbed Pluto after his faithful Persian cat, and his name quickly became a household word.

Franz was born in Chicago in 1906 and grew up on a small farm in central Illinois on the outskirts of Peoria. He was tall, lanky, with dark-brown hair and black eyes. He was his parents' first and only child.

Franz was a precocious boy. When he was ten years old, he spent the evening hours in his parents' backyard, gazing at the stars and drawing the constellations in a black spiral notebook. At the age of fifteen he built a three-inch f/10 refractor telescope out of spare parts from his father's garage. He even ground the lenses himself. His father had always harbored a laymen's interest in astronomy and took great delight in his son's budding interest.

Franz attended Rockmore High School where he felt at home with the school's science and mathematics curriculum. He had exhausted the school's math offerings by his senior year and took Advanced Calculus and Number Theory at Bradley University. Even with such a demanding course of study, he maintained a straight A average and became Rockmore's valedictorian in 1924, an honor which landed him a four-year scholarship to New Mexico State University.

It was at State where he met his future bride, Isabella Rutherford, a pretty girl with wavy brown hair and joyful eyes. He pursued her with an unrelenting passion, and after a dizzying courtship, they were married in the university chapel.

Franz completed his bachelor's degree in physics and astronomy with highest honors and, after a short stint at an aerospace firm in Chicago, applied for a job at Lowell Observatory in Flagstaff, Arizona. He sent the observatory a series of photographs he had taken of Jupiter and Saturn. If the truth be told, he was merely hoping for a critique of his work. To his surprise, he was offered a position as a research associate.

The project to which he was assigned involved the search for a mysterious "Planet X," a rumored planetary body that lay somewhere beyond Neptune, a search begun in 1905 by Percival Lowell, a search which in a quarter of a century had gone nowhere. His job involved scanning the heavens with the aid of the observatory's thirteen-inch f/5 photographic camera. Working in the cold, unheated dome, Franz made pairs of exposures of portions of the sky with time intervals of two to six days. These were scrutinized under a device called a Blink Comparator in hopes of detecting a small shift in position of one of the hundreds of thousands of points of light—the sign of a planet among a field of stars.

On the nights of January 23 and 29, 1930, Franz made two such photographs of the region around the star Delta Geminorum in the constellation of Gemini. On the afternoon of January 31, comparing the plates with the Blink Comparator, he detected the telltale shift of a faint, starlike image: a fourteen-magnitude speck of light shifting from plate to plate exactly as a planet should have done. The discovery was confirmed with subsequent observations and announced to the world on March 13, 1930.

Soon Franz found himself crisscrossing the country, giving talks at prominent colleges and universities. He delighted in recounting the tale of his planetary discovery, which he compared to finding a needle in a haystack. It was tedious work, he said, but better than pitching hay on his father's farm.

He moved to Arizona five months later where he began work on a PhD in astronomy at the University of Arizona, receiving a degree five years later from the Department of Astronomy and Astrophysics. He returned to Lowell as a Senior Scientist and was given his own research group. Working literally thousands of hours over the next ten years, he discovered three star clusters, a dozen asteroids, and several comets. He also developed a disturbing taste for alcohol, which he and his associates would imbibe late into the evenings, much to his wife's dismay.

He left the observatory in 1945 for a position at Harvard University. His future was full of promise. The sky was the limit, he said with a grin that stretched from ear to ear. He was thirty-nine years old.

Franz and Isabella arrived in Boston on August 7, 1945. They rented a two-bedroom apartment a short walk from campus. He taught a class on the dynamics of the solar system during the fall semester. It was enormously popular. Several departmental lectures were also well-received. His future at Harvard seemed assured.

Franz was known to frequent the bars in Watertown and had a particular fondness for Irish ale. One evening around ten, after having quaffed several pints, he refilled his glass, raised it high over his head, and cried out in a booming voice, "Long live Galileo!" Everyone laughed—somewhat nervously, if the truth be told, for Franz had a demonic look about him—and it was then he noticed a pretty brunette with green eyes staring at him from across the room. He smiled, his eyes rolled slowly back, and then everything went black. It was late December and a gentle snow was falling.

When he came to he was in Massachusetts General Hospital. A young nurse was fluttering around his bed. Her white uniform was immaculate. She seemed unbearably happy. She looked at Franz and smiled.

Franz did not know what to think. His head ached and his ears were ringing. He wished he was dreaming though he knew he was not. He closed his eyes and his mind drifted off. He felt as if he was walking down a long, dark tunnel, the floor of which was covered with a brown moss soft as velvet. And then it was if he was on another world, one of Saturn's moons perhaps. Or some other place. His mind was lost in an impenetrable fog.

"What happened?" he asked when he emerged from his daydream.

"You drank too much," the nurse said. "You fell and hit your head. You were knocked unconscious."

"Oh."

"You're lucky, you know. It could have been worse. I hope you learned a lesson."

He looked around the room. It must have been early morning for a dappled sunlight was streaming in through the window. There was another bed in the room but it was empty. A coatrack in one corner. Two seascapes on the wall facing him, one of which looked vaguely familiar.

Another nurse came in, carrying a white clipboard. She had a hawk-like nose and her graying brown hair was tied up in a bun. She glared at Franz as if his mere presence was an aggravation.

"Name?" She fairly spit out the word.

It was then he realized that he did not know who he was.

$$* * *$$

Amnesia is memory loss caused either by physical injury to the brain or by the ingestion of a toxic substance which affects the brain. In addition, it can be caused by a traumatic, emotional event. In Franz's case, it was most likely due to his longtime consumption of alcohol and the recent blow to his head. When he had been admitted to the hospital, he was disoriented and confused, and was hysterical when questioned.

The doctors explained it all to a frightened Isabella who had been summoned to the emergency room in the dead of night. The woman's voice on the other end of the line had sounded positively ghostly. Isabella called a cab to take her to the hospital. The wind was howling like a pack of wolves. When she arrived, her eyes were shining with tears.

Had Franz ever had an epileptic seizure?

Isabella shook her head, no.

Was there a history of epilepsy in his family?

Not that she was aware of.

Had there been psychological trauma in the recent past?

Again, no. He had been working hard, ever since his days at the observatory, and probably was overdue for a vacation. But he simply would not rest. And then there was the drinking which she admitted she had known about for some time.

Psychotherapy could be helpful for people whose amnesia was caused by emotional trauma, they told her. For instance, hypnosis might help some patients recall forgotten memories. Occasionally it was appropriate to administer drugs.

No, Isabella said, Franz would have nothing to do with them.

The length of the amnesia was variable depending upon the cause of the memory problem. By removing the toxic substance, for instance alcohol, the person's memory would probably recover within a short period of time. However, if the brain had been more severely injured—as was the case with her husband—it might take months or even years for a complete recovery to occur. In some instances, the amnesia never went away.

Oh dear, she said. That would never do.

Three days later Franz was moved to the rehabilitation ward. To the surprise of everyone, his amnesia was steadily abating. The doctors said their initial prognosis was in error, that his case was less severe than first thought, and that in a matter of days he would undoubtedly be fine.

Unfortunately, it was not a matter of days. Franz's early progress slowed to a crawl after the first week and at one point he even seemed to regress. His treatment consisted of a stringent set of memory exercises administered three times a day. A psychologist shot question after question at the astronomer in a vain attempt to probe his memory. At one point the psychologist said there was nothing more he could do and discharged the patient (in reality, he thought Franz was not taking the treatment seriously). And it was then that Franz began to recover. It was a slow and agonizing process. But at least this time it was for real.

Franz returned to Harvard after six months at the rehabilitation center. It was the fall of 1946. A lavish party was thrown in his honor in the great ballroom of Municipal

Hall. One by one the members of the astronomy department congratulated him on his recovery. It was truly remarkable, they said. And it was.

Franz danced late into the night with Isabella, who was wearing a pink evening gown and white slippers. Around 2 AM he gave a speech thanking everyone for a wonderful evening. The crystal chandelier that hung in the center of the ballroom glittered splendidly as he spoke, and there were tears in his eyes as he painstakingly described his time at the rehabilitation center. The days when he thought he would never be able to conduct research again. His speech was slurred, a fact people attributed to one too many drinks.

* * *

Franz taught one class that semester: Introduction to Astronomy for Non-Majors. There were eighty students. He began the course with great enthusiasm—it felt so good to lecture once again—and his students found his love of the material infectious. But several weeks into the semester something strange occurred. He was discussing the spectral qualities of Type A stars when without warning he realized he could no longer speak. He stared blankly at the students and reached for the glass of water on his desk. He felt faint. The awkward silence was broken when a girl in the front row asked a question about Hertzsprung-Russell diagrams and he was somehow able to recover. But the incident left him shaken and confused.

"You came back too soon," the chairman said later that day. "But it's nothing to be ashamed of. It happens to the best of us." He told Franz to take the rest of the semester off. He needed to make a complete recovery before resuming the rigors of academic life. Franz started to protest, but the chairman brushed him off. "It will be better for all of us," he said. Franz did as requested.

The following semester Franz taught two classes and resumed his research on asteroids, but he was clearly not himself. People began to talk behind his back. It was generally agreed that he had not recovered. One colleague—a man who had always envied Franz—said out loud that Franz was a nutcase. At his yearly physical, Franz mentioned periods of forgetfulness. The physician was aware of Franz's history but assured him that such periods were normal for a recovering amnesiac. Nevertheless, Franz told the doctor, he was concerned. Isabella had mentioned the possibility of epilepsy.

The doctor asked if there was a history of epilepsy in Franz's family.

He shook his head, no.

Had he ever blacked out before?

No.

Suffered from convulsions?

Definitely not.

Did he experience periods of forgetfulness or confusion?

Not that he was aware of.

Was he ever unable to talk or communicate for short periods of time?

Now that the doctor mentioned it, there had been several episodes when he was in his twenties.

Of a transient nature?

Yes.

The doctor chuckled. Merely the last gasps of an extended adolescence, he said. Franz worried too much.

Perhaps.

Had there been any occurrences in recent years?

Franz hesitated; he realized that to tell the truth invited ridicule. No, he said.

The doctor thumped Franz on his back and told him to relax. But Franz was not reassured.

* * *

Franz tried to publish—one article on the chemical composition of the rings of Saturn, another on the orbital characteristics of the moons of Jupiter—but his ideas were rejected. His lectures became increasingly incoherent and attendance in his classes dwindled.

His appointment was not renewed. The vote was unanimous. It was the beginning of the end. He was permitted to lecture for the remainder of the academic year, but then would have to find other employment. One dreary evening he and Isabella had a ferocious argument. She left him shortly thereafter. She wanted nothing to do with a failure, she said angrily, though the reason was something else entirely. (She was having an affair with one of Franz's colleagues.) Nothing in his life could have prepared Franz for this. It left him broken-hearted, and he even contemplated suicide.

In the fall of 1947, he took a job at the White Sands Proving Ground in New Mexico, a position granted him at the request of the head of the astronomy department at Harvard. His job was to develop the optical tracking system for a new telescope. He was dismissed two years later, ostensibly for financial reasons, but actually because he had accomplished nothing.

He returned to Illinois and bought a small house on the outskirts of Peoria, five miles from his boyhood home. Over the next year he assembled a twelve-inch reflecting telescope made of parts from a local surplus store and built an observatory to house it in his backyard.

He obtained a job at the local library. He spent his days shelving books and at night studied the heavens from the haven of his observatory. He was searching for a nova in the constellation Corvus. Gienah—the bird in flight—a third-magnitude star about four times the diameter of the Sun surrounded by an expanding shell of material expelled from the star. It was a theory he had postulated at Harvard the year before he left—a nova to arise in that minor constellation—but which had been summarily dismissed by his colleagues. Gienah did not have the required spectral properties for a nova, they insisted. His idea was mere fancy.

When he had been at Lowell in the waning months of 1929, Franz thought he had detected such a nova—a bluish speck against the vaulted dome of the night—and had noted it in his plate log one evening. But then Pluto appeared and he had not had the time to investigate further. When he reviewed the plates months later he found nothing; the event had yet to occur.

Franz made more than 1000 photographic plates in the years 1951-1960. The nights were long and lonely, but he did not mind. He was conducting important research once again. Let them think me worthless, he thought, as he stared bleary-eyed at the latest photographic plate. What does it matter?

Unfortunately, he did not find what he was searching for. It had been so long ago. Perhaps he was mistaken. Perhaps it was something else that he had seen. This, he had to admit, was possible: his amnesia's final insult.

He built a second scope, a sixteen-inch reflector of his own design. Over the next decade he made nightly observations, photographing nearly sixty-five percent of the night sky. He came upon a multitude of magnificent objects—galaxies, nebulae, planets, comets, quasars, constellations, and a variety of interstellar oddities—but no nova.

Eventually he returned to Corvus, that constellation he knew so well. And it was on December 23, 1971 when he again noted the telltale sign of a nova in outburst. Subsequent observations confirmed the finding this time. *Al Janah al Ghurab al Aiman*, the Right Wing of the Raven, had revealed itself to him.

At Harvard they had thought him a scientific failure. His wife thought him a failure as a man. Even at White Sands in a job that—he must be honest with himself—was little more than a technician's, he had failed miserably.

All that was behind him now. He had made amends. *He had shown that the discovery of Pluto had not been a fluke*. He locked up the observatory and walked down the gravel path that led to his house. He took the heavy photographic plate —the plate that recorded his new discovery—and tossed it into the fireplace. And with a dreamy sigh, he got into bed and soon was fast asleep.

* * *

It is not known what happened to Franz at this point for he was never heard from again. When the cleaning lady came the next Saturday (it was the only indulgence he allowed himself) the house was empty. Mrs. Brooks saw the burnt-out coals in the fireplace, his bed all made-up, the refrigerator full. She sensed something was wrong and she alerted the police. "Name sounds familiar," the officer-in-charge said as he pushed his spectacles up the bridge of his nose, but he couldn't remember where he'd heard it before. The police investigation turned up nothing of importance. Franz had no debts, no enemies, no contact with anyone, actually. No one knew what he did if anything. He was the epitome of a recluse. The police filed a missing persons report with the state authorities and that was the end of the matter.

"Looks like I need another job," Mrs. Brooks said to her husband the next day. "And we're going to have to cut back for a while." Her husband had suffered a stroke several years before and was unable to work. It had fallen on her to provide for him and their two children.

"Trouble is, there's not much out there these days."

The cleaning lady had always liked her employer. Unlike others, Franz was considerate and kind. Perhaps he had traveled west to Montana where the skies were reputed to be immense, she thought. He was always talking about the stars. Or maybe he had simply vanished from the earth, the sands of his hourglass having run out.

There had been one other thing. She hadn't mentioned it to the police because, well, it simply slipped her mind. A scrap of paper, probably unimportant, which she'd found on his desk after he'd disappeared. It read like the answer to a riddle. A riddle which itself was unknown. She smiled as she held it in her hands and read. Somehow it seemed quite fitting:

> My mother held the sky,
> My father all the stars;
> And me, I am a child of God,
> One day I'll travel far.

Nothing of significance ever came of the missing persons report and Franz's whereabouts were to forever remain a mystery.

THE ROOM AT THE END OF THE WORLD

(undated)

There is a door at the end of the hall. You open it and see a second door. You open that and see a third. When you open this door, you are not surprised to see a fourth. You continue stepping inside and opening doors. You do this for a long, long time. At some point in this repetitive process you realize that each door has been painted a different color. You have no idea why this is so, but you find it interesting. A while later you realize that not only is each door a different color, but that the colors are following in order the colors of the spectrum: shades of red, orange, yellow, green, blue, and violet, and that each color is more brilliant, more radiant, than the one before. It is indeed an interesting phenomenon. It never occurs to you that you might be lost and had better go back, and it is a good thing this does not occur to you, for if you were to turn around you would see that there are no doors behind you, that they are dissolving into nothingness the moment you step through them. At last you reach what you believe must be the final door. It is painted a brilliant white and it is so bright you must cover your eyes to keep from being blinded as you open the door. You expect to see a stately room, for it has been your experience that all doors lead to rooms and if one must pass through many doors to reach a room it must be because it is a very stately room indeed, or if not a room perhaps another door, this being a labyrinth into which you have stumbled and from which you shall never escape. But you see neither a room nor a door. You see nothing. Emptiness. The void. You are at a loss. Taking a deep breath, which you realize may well be your last, you step through the door. Nothing happens (did you really expect something to happen?), only another door appears and you step through this one, too.

The End

ABOUT THE AUTHOR

Brian Biswas has published dozens of stories in the United States as well as internationally. He is the author of the short story collection *A Betrayal and Other Stories*. He writes in a literary style reminiscent of magical realism which attempts to convey a slightly exaggerated but internally consistent sense of reality. He also writes gothic or neo-gothic tales, and straightforward horror and science fiction stories, often tinged with fantastic elements.

Brian was born in Columbus, Ohio. He received a B.A. in Philosophy from Antioch College in Yellow Springs, Ohio, and an M.S. in Computer Science from the University of Illinois at Urbana-Champaign. He lives in an old neighborhood in Chapel Hill, North Carolina with his wife, Elizabeth, and an ever-changing assortment of animals.

ABOUT THE PUBLISHER

Whisk(e)y Tit is committed to restoring degradation and degeneracy to the literary arts. We work with authors who are unwilling to sacrifice intellectual rigor, unrelenting playfulness, and visual beauty in our literary pursuits, often leading to texts that would otherwise be abandoned in today's largely homogenized literary landscape. In a world governed by idiocy, our commitment to these principles is an act of civil service and civil disobedience alike.